The Christmas Beagle

S.E. Eaton

For Steven and Emmie Lou
Special thanks to Mom

Table of Contents

Chapter One

June 7th, 2007

gretagal45@courtingconnection.wuf

to: me

Confession time, Al! My wonderful grandson set this up for me but I still have little idea what I'm doing! Slowly I am figuring this thing out, but I have much more to learn about interacting online. Let me get right to it: I saw your picture and read your online bio. After all I've been through these past few months it was a blessing to run across someone like you. You have two grandchildren, right? I have four grandchildren myself, two grandsons and two granddaughters. They all live out-of-state so I don't get to see them as much as I'd like. I spend a lot of my time alone, though I do make it to church now and then. I know firsthand it can be difficult to meet the right person, especially in the "golden years". …Even more so after being married to the same person for decades. But I'm ready to enjoy life again. I'm ready for companionship. I'm ready to find someone to eat my too-large batches of oatmeal cookies! (After raising a family, you never do get used to cooking for one!) Hope we can get to know each other better.

Talk to you soon, Al.

Take care,

-Greta

June 10th, 2007

albertcole123@courtingconnection.wuf

to: me

Greta,

Thank you for your message.   Your profile didn't say where you live…are you in Oregon? You mentioned you've had a rough go of it lately…hope things start looking up for you. I'll confess, too…this is my first time using the internet for this purpose. At 78 years old, I never thought I'd have much need for it. But I miss having someone to talk to. It took my granddaughter all weekend just to teach me how to "sign in".

My family lives close-by, but even so, I don't see them much, except for my granddaughter. She's a peach--- named after me, "Alexandria". I'd love to get to know you better, too. You mentioned on your page you like Italian food. Maybe I could take you out for a nice meal sometime. What's your favorite dish?   Talk to you soon.

Albert C.

Chapter Two

December, 2011

The windshield yelped as Pete dragged the squeegee down the length of it. He watched, with uneasy eyes, as brown water trickled down into the crack of the hood. His hands ached from the cold as he tucked his utensils under his arm and smiled at the customer behind the wheel. She rolled down her window no more than two inches and leaned up towards the gap. Pete jutted his chin to hear her. "I'm not paying you," she said. She gave a sharp forward gesture. "You left dirt streaks all over my windshield!"

Pete rubbed his mustache and breathed out a puff of white winter air. He gritted his teeth and made himself mindful of the envelope inside his pocket. With a frown, he looked at the customer. "…Real sorry about that, Ma'am. Little low on cleaning solution today." The faint sound of muffled music came from the backseat, where two other people, a teenage boy and a young girl sat. Headphones arched over the boy's head and colored lights from the girl's handheld device lit up her stony face. Pete felt the woman's glare tearing into him. He pulled his eyes away from her kids. "I understand," he said. "…Happy Holidays. Y'all take care, now."

The woman's nose twitched. *"Merry Christmas,"* she said. She rolled up her window and sped off from the intersection, her back tire dousing Pete's legs in a wave of muddy ice water. His sodden pants stuck to his shins and released prickles of cold up and down his body.

He watched with glossed-over eyes as the car disappeared into the busy city streets. Through the rear window, he caught sight of the young girl looking back at him. Pete sighed. "Merry Christmas, Ma'am." He tucked the trigger of his water-filled spray bottle into the waistband of his sweatpants, shoved the squeegee into his sweatshirt, walked down an alley and ducked behind a dumpster. Wedging his thumb into his pants pocket, he thrust his other hand inside it and pulled out a few wrinkled dollar bills as well as other items, a marble, a paperclip, a faded puzzle piece, and a glue stick cap. He reached into his back pocket and pulled out a fat envelope that was folded in half. The squeegee slipped out from inside his sweatshirt and clattered on the damp cement. Pete nudged it to one side with his toe. His numb hands shaking from the cold, he traced his fingers along the front of the envelope, where the words *Grace Fund* were written. He secured the money inside the envelope.

Evening crept into the alley. Pete sat up against the wall and reached under the dumpster, pulling out a stack of newspapers, each of which were at least two years old. He glanced at the headline on the top paper. *House Fire Kills Three*. He arranged the newspapers around him and fell asleep with his head bowed between his knees. Several hours later, a cold, wet sensation on his neck woke him. He jerked his head back, wincing as he slammed it against the bricks behind him. He groaned but permitted understanding as the smell of damp dog met his nose. A beagle, her tail in a furious wag, grinned at Pete. "Ah...it's you!" Pete said, rubbing the dog's ears. "Hungry little beagle, I bet?" The beagle cocked her head and licked her chops. "Sorry, girl, I don't have any food on me. But let's see what we can do to fix that, hmm?"

Chapter Three

June 10th, 2007

gretagal45@courtingconnection.wuf

to: me

Al,

I live in Arizona. Been here for ten years, but was born and raised in Houston. Moved here with my late husband after our business went south.

Dinner sometime sounds lovely, should we ever meet! When I was a little girl, my great-grandmother taught me how to make her famous spaghetti sauce. It's my family's best kept secret. My mother warned me to never tell anyone outside the family what it is. If I wanted to, I could make a lot of money selling the stuff---I don't mean to brag, but it's that good! Alright, maybe I'm a little biased. I did grow up on the stuff. I value my mother's wishes, though, more than I value money. Oh, listen to me, rambling on without answering your question! Spaghetti is my answer, made of course, with my great-grandmother's recipe. If we hit it off, I'd love to make it for you sometime.

You're lucky to have your granddaughter. Cherish her...you never know when your family will be taken from you, even the young ones. I usually don't tell people this unless I've know them for quite some time, but I lost my son to cancer when he was nineteen. That was many years ago, but not a day goes by where I don't think of him. He was going to be a doctor.

Tell me more about you! Are you retired? What line of work were you in? Retirement can be rough. They say our minds start to go south if we've nothing to do, and Lord knows social security isn't what it used to be.

Wishing you a wonderful day, Al.

-Greta B.

Chapter Four

December, 2011

Aaron's feet crunched the frosted gravel as he strolled through the car lot. The 1994 Toyota brought him to a stop, its black veneer inciting a gleam in his eye. He stared at the window sticker and narrowed his eyes. "Soon," he said. He clenched his fists and grinned. "...*Soon.*"

Two figures appeared in his periphery. He turned his head. One, the salesman, was dressed in a shirt and tie, and was escorting the other away from the cars.

"Didn't mean to cause any trouble," the other said. "I was only hoping for a cup of your fresh coffee to warm my hands."

"Then go get a job, lazy bum!" the salesperson said. He frowned as he looked to Aaron, as though sizing him up, then turned around and gave his attention to a couple who were looking at a hybrid car a few rows from Aaron.

Aaron glanced at the homeless man. He remembered seeing him around town before, including an unfortunate incident involving Aaron's irate mother. He had given him money from time to time, though Aaron doubted the man remembered him. "That was brutal, dude," Aaron said. "That guy's a jerk."

The man gave a dismissive wave. "Ah, he's harmless." He nodded to the Toyota. "That's a mighty fine piece of machinery."

Aaron grinned and slid his fingertips into his pockets. "...Play my cards right, it'll be mine, next month."

"Excellent taste," the man said. "…You saving up?"

Aaron nodded. "Yes, Sir." He wrinkled his brow and gave a tight smile. "…Aghh, almost there, too! I turn sixteen next month. Going to get my license on my birthday, then come and make this bad boy mine."

"That's a good goal," the man said. "But you know what this truck needs?" he asked. Aaron gave a hesitant smirk and shook his head. "A dog," the man said. "A pretty little hound. And it just so happens I have *access* to such a companion. She's been following me around for weeks now…she'll disappear now and then, but always comes back, looking for a belly scratch and a scrap of food. Blessed thing made me some good money, what with her dance moves and those beggin' eyes of hers, but she deserves what I can't give her. ….Warmth…security…a *home*. Wouldn't charge anything for her, only because she's priceless, and well, she isn't really mine to sell…." He narrowed one eye and looked at Aaron. "You interested? You look like the type to offer a lot of love to a little beagle."

"Oh…" Aaron said, shaking his head. "Sorry, but, uh…we're not really…pet *people*…? My family, I mean. We don't really have the time to take care of them. Um…good luck, though, I uh…hope you find a good home for her."

The man nodded. He gave a wary glance to the lot office. "I better get out of here before he calls the police. Happy Holidays, man," he said, nodding to Aaron. "Good luck with your truck."

Aaron frowned and dug his hand into his pocket, pulling out his wallet. "…Wait, uh…." The man turned around and scratched his chin. "Here," Aaron said, holding out a ten dollar bill to the man.

The man frowned at the money. "Well now, I can't take money from a man with a savings plan! That truck needs an owner!"

Aaron shrugged. "Been saving since I was fourteen." He pressed the money into the man's hand. "I've got plenty, really." He reached back into his pocket and emptied his loose change on top of the bill.

The man smiled. "Well...God bless you."

A clump of gray fluff nestled within the change caught Aaron's eye. He cringed. "Oops...sorry, you, uh, probably don't want pocket lint." He retrieved the fluff and tucked it back into his pocket.

"Been given worse," the man said. "...All sorts of odds and ends. People don't pay much mind to what they're givin' me, I guess. But I don't mind it. Amongst their junk I often find treasure, and I'm not referring to the money."

Aaron gave a small smile. "Heh...yeah, no...I get that. Well anyways...see you around. I've got to get back home...supposed to babysit my sister tonight. Happy Holidays."

The man nodded. "Take care, truck man."

Chapter Five

June 12th, 2007

albertcole123@courtingconnection.wuf

to: me

Greta,

I worked for many years as a lawyer. And actually, I'm blessed to have a cozy retirement. The title denotes high wages, and I certainly did alright, but if it weren't for my wife's handsome life insurance policy, I'd not be doing as well as I am. I was a spender, and the worst of them, to boot. Linda was a saver and I thank God for that. It's rubbed off on me, somewhat, but I have my weak moments, mostly involving fine dining and spoiling my granddaughter. I live in a small apartment, but it works for my simplistic lifestyle.

As for minds going south, I've got something to say on the matter. I'm sharp as a tack, I swear up and down I am, but my family (Lexi excluded) thinks I've lost my mind. …And they're basing this, mind you, because I bought two gallons of milk last week instead of one. They tell me my mind is slipping, but what they don't know because they refused to listen is that I was going to give the other gallon to Lexi because she's always talking about running out of milk for her coffee. She works as a waitress and struggles from time to time. My point is, there's nothing wrong with me. I'm retired, but I read and garden; plenty of activity to keep my noggin engaged! You come off as intelligent, too, Greta. I'm certain you are, and if I might say, you look very beautiful in your photos. You're a classic beauty, as they say.

Have a good day,

Albert C.

Chapter Six

December, 2011

Hannah pushed her thumb against the Vega star puzzle piece, conjoining it with the Lyra constellation. In her periphery, she looked at her mom. "...But I don't *want* to move. I *like* it here."

Mom bit her lip, frowning as she made a notation on the rolled-out blueprint on the kitchen table. "The apartment was always temporary, Hannah, remember? Remember our plan? We live in the city for the duration of my big project, then we buy a plot of land and build our own house."

A small crease formed on Hannah's forehead. "But I don't want to move. *I like it here.*"

"Well...it isn't up for discussion, Hannah," Mom said. "This time next year we will be in a house in the suburbs. Just think of how much fun it will be to decorate for Christmas! We can have a banister, decorated with real cedar swags, just like my mom had when I was a kid." Mom glanced to one side. "Uh, well, fake but *realistic* cedar swags, so the smell doesn't bother you."

"But I don't want to move," Hannah said. "I'm not going to move. You and Aaron can move. I'm not going to move."

Mom sighed. "I know that's how you *feel*, Hannah."

"No, Mom, that's not right," Hannah said. "Not moving isn't a feeling. Being *angry* because your mom wants to take you away from your home and *change* everything is a feeling. But I'm not angry. I'm just not *moving*."

The front door opened. Hannah's brother Aaron walked in, carrying with him a burst of cold. Hannah rubbed the goose bumps from her arms while Aaron pulled his headphones from his ears and gave a meager smile to his family.

"I'm not moving," Hannah said. "Aaron, you and Mom are moving. I'm staying here."

Mom gave a distracted wave to Aaron, pursing her lips together as she looked back to Hannah. "...How about this? We can talk more about moving later, after you show me that new telescope you want for Christmas? And on the way home we can stop for ice cream, or hot cocoa, or whatever you want."

"What I want," Hannah said, "is to *not move*. I don't want ice cream. I don't want hot cocoa. And I don't..." she said, pounding both fists on the table, "*want to move!*"

Mom gave a thin smile. "Well, *yes*, Sweetie, but..."

"NO!" Hannah shouted. Mom opened her mouth, closed it, sighed and folded her hands on the table top.

Aaron scowled at Hannah. "Stop yelling at Mom, jeeze! You're moving whether you like it or not, so get over it already!"

Hannah burned holes into Aaron's face as she glared at him. "Shut up! *I'm not moving*! YOU CAN MOVE!"

Mom sighed. "Both of you, stop!"

"Good," Aaron said, ignoring Mom. "Stay here and scream at no one when you don't get your way. Mom and I will enjoy some peace and quiet for once!"

Mom put up her hand. "Aaron…! *Don't*." She cast a wary glance towards Hannah, who, although her cheeks flushed red, had refocused her angry energy on her puzzle. She moved her hand in quick, jerky motions to retrieve the pieces, and hammered them into place with her fist.

Aaron shot his brow upwards and shrugged. "Mom, come on! She doesn't need to scream bloody murder every time she doesn't like something or doesn't get her way! It's stupid and obnoxious…not to mention *rude*. Get her meds upped, or something."

"I take enough medicine," Hannah said. "My doctor said so. If it wasn't enough, she would give me more. But she hasn't given me more, so it's *enough*."

"Oh, yeah," Aaron said. "And I'm sure a doctor could never be wrong, right? Don't be stupid, Hannah."

Hannah looked up at her brother, her face void of emotion. "I'm not stupid. I am extremely intelligent."

"Not about some things, you're not," Aaron said. "For example, if you think you're staying here while Mom and me move, then you're *incredibly* stupid."

"HEY!" Mom shouted, while Hannah's balled fists trembled as she broke into a high-pitched screech.

"I'M. NOT. *MOVING*!" Hannah shouted. Her face turned purple.

Mom's voice shook with a careful tension. "*Puzzle!*" she said, scooting the unfinished work towards Hannah. Her voice took on a slowed, subdued tone. "…Incomplete puzzle, just *waiting* to be done, Sweetie. Don't you want to finish it?" Hannah dropped her shoulders, unfurled her clenched muscles and resumed placing puzzle pieces together.

Mom's jaw twitched as she glared at Aaron. Aaron scowled. "...Whatever." He shuffled down the hall, shouted a swear word, and slammed his door shut.

Hannah kept her eyes glued to her work as she pointed towards the hall. "Bad word, *bad word*!"

Mom buried her face into her hands, groaned, looked up, flipped her hair off her shoulder and walked down the hall. Hannah put another puzzle piece into place.

Mom's waspish tone carried down the hall. "Hey! That little display of yours was *completely* uncalled for! What's your problem?"

Hannah couldn't decipher Aaron's response, but it sounded low, the way it did when Mom accused him of being sarcastic. Hannah had to push a little more to get the next puzzle piece to fit.

"I asked you a question, Aaron."

Aaron's tone shifted to an octave higher.

"Don't give me that!" Mom said.

An unintelligible rumble sounded once more.

"That's no excuse!" Mom said, "*You can't go around purposefully setting her off like that*!" Hannah heard Aaron push out a dramatic sigh and say her name. She rubbed her thumb against the smooth surface of the puzzle piece in her hand, though the smudge on it had already disappeared.

"It's not all her fault!" Mom said. "Right now this is about you and your attitude!"

More sarcastic rumbling. Hannah hammered her fist against the stubborn puzzle piece. It slid into place.

"I don't like your tone!" Mom said. "Change it, and change your attitude or you and I are going to have a *real* problem on our hands."

Hannah scanned the coffee table top for the last puzzle piece. It wasn't there. She looked under the couch and coffee table. She shook the box, but found it empty. The scream inside her stirred. She closed her eyes, balled her fists and said through clenched teeth, "Ten, nine, eight, seven...." She whimpered as the scream pounded at the back of her throat. "I'm trying! I'm trying! I'm *trying*!" she said. She took in several shaky breaths. "...Six...five...four...three...two...one...." With a mournful pout, she looked at the unfinished puzzle. The scream, instead of through her voice, came out of her hands, as, with her face twisted and tears in her eyes, she smacked the puzzle off the table. It hit the wall and fell to the floor, most of it intact. Hannah sent a reproachful glare towards the hall, from where Aaron shouted back at Mom. She thrust hands to her ears and sobbed.

Chapter Seven

June 15th, 2007

gretagal45@courtingconnection.wuf

to: me

Al,

You devil, you made me blush! Thank you for the compliments. I understand about family disagreements. Last month, after my car accident, my son (not the one I lost to cancer) said he was too busy to come and visit me. Now, I understand, he lives out of state and works full time, has a family of his own, etc, but what hurts is that my friend Susan ran into him at the grocery store the next day! He was in town for a friend's bachelor party but couldn't take the time to come and see his mom. He's not a bad person, but I was shocked to think that I raised someone who would make such a choice. I got hit by a drunk driver, got pretty banged up but am healing alright now. Doc says when I finish physical therapy in a couple of weeks I should be back to normal.

A lawyer! Well, that's something to be proud of, Al! I was a waitress most of my life at a little diner in Houston. Don't have much of a retirement, but I get along alright. I, too, like to send my extra money to my kids, make sure they have all they need, etc. I guess one never stops being a mother!

Don't let your family push you around, but keep in mind, they love you. No matter what, they love you.

Take care.

Fondly,

-Greta B.

Chapter Eight

December, 2011

Tray in one hand and a wet towel in the other, Alex wiped her wrist across her forehead, wincing as spasms of pain shot up and down her neck and right shoulder blade. She rolled her shoulders several times and loaded the dirty cups and plates onto the tray. Out of the corner of her eye, she saw a couple enter the diner, holding on to each other like the other might float away any moment. Alex, her smile thin, pushed out a curt sigh through her nose, angling her aching body away from them. The man in the next booth waved at her.

Alex rested the tray on her hip and smiled at the man. "What can I do for you?"

"Back hurtin' ya?" the man said.

"Yup," Alex said. "…Same as it always has."

The man chuckled. "Aw, come on now! You're too young to have back pain! What in the world happened to make it hurt? …You fall?"

Alex gave a tight smile. "You've never worked in the food service industry, have you, Sir?"

The man frowned and rubbed the handle of his coffee cup. "Well, *no*, but…."

Alex sighed. "To answer your question, the enormity of life and all its horrors happened to it."

The man frowned, as though Alex's answer offended him on a personal level. "Well, no sense in focusing on it. It'll only make it worse, you know."

Alex shook her head. "I don't focus on it. But I don't pretend it's not happening, either. There are plenty of happy things in my life I can focus on. And I do."

"Good!" the man said. "That's what's important, after all." He pointed at her. "That's what really matters. If you focused on the blessings even more, I bet you'd find your back pain isn't nearly as bad as you think it is."

Alex turned away from the man, feigning interest in a baby in the booth behind her. She rolled her eyes and sighed. Digging her nails into the underside of the tray and plastering on a smile, she looked to the man again. "Anything I can get you, Sir?" She cocked her head to one side and made her smile grow. "...Refill on your coffee?"

"No, no...I'm fine, Miss," the man said. "Thank you! ...And Merry Christmas! Oh, I mean...Happy Holidays! ...Not supposed to say Merry Christmas, you know, never know who you're gonna offend!"

"Yup," Alex said. Her jaw tightened. "You never do know, do you? Happy Holidays to you, too, Sir."

"Miss...? Miss! *Hey!*" Alex looked over her shoulder. A curvaceous woman with a mound of curls and caked-on makeup shook a ketchup bottle at her. "*It's empty, dear!*"

"Be right with you!" Alex said. She sighed through her teeth. "*What I won't put up with to keep the lights turned on....*" She took swift strides towards the customer, but stopped short as her manager stepped into her path. "Oops, sorry, Mary...."

"Alex...favor to ask you," Mary said. As though there were a rotten taste on her tongue, she scrunched her lips and leaned in close to Alex's ear. Alex could see the makeup lines along her jaw line. She did her best to not wrinkle her nose as Mary's flowery perfume and coffee breath assaulted her nostrils. "There's a homeless gentleman sitting outside on the sidewalk….?" Mary pushed out an impertinent sigh. "It's just, well, we can't have that...*kind of person*...associated with our establishment. *I need you to go out there and ask him to move along.*"

Alex took a half-step back away from her. "Uh...sure thing. I just...a customer needs ketchup, so…"

"Take care of that, then take care of the...*other thing*," Mary said. She squinted as she smiled and patted Alex's arm. "I appreciate you following through on that for me." She left, revealing the ketchup customer behind her, who stared at Alex.

"*Hello...?*" the customer said. "Dear...? Ketchup...? You do have actual ketchup in this diner, right? I don't suppose this empty bottle is nothing but a prop?"

Alex yanked the empty bottle from the customer's hand, offered a forced, bright smile and started for the kitchen, where she unloaded the tray and refilled the ketchup bottle. On her way back, she caught a glimpse through the front window of the homeless man, as well as a small crowd that had gathered. The crowd laughed and clapped. A hesitant smile on her face, Alex left the ketchup bottle on a random table, ignored the confused inquiry written on the face from the customer sitting there, and made her way to the exit.

Alex rolled up on her toes to see over the mountainous shoulder of a man and looked at the homeless man. "Now who has some music for us?" he said. "Sing a song, and this pretty girl here will dance for you!" The tall man in front of her shifted to the right, blocking a proper view.

A little boy started to sing, off-key but with a jovial force, "*Jingle Bells, Jingle Bells, Jingle all the way!*" A few others joined in, and after a moment, so did Alex. She wiggled her way in front of the men, chuckling when she saw the dancer, a beagle, up on her hind legs. The beagle turned in circles, howling and yipping along with the music. The song tapered off half-way through when the beagle sat, and the crowd clapped as the homeless man gave her a treat.

A few people pressed dollar bills into the man's hand. He gave a series of curt nods as he pocketed the money. "Thank you...thank you," he said. The crowd dispersed.

Alex picked a few paint flakes from her fingernails and smiled at the homeless man. He blinked and stared at her, as though surprised at her acknowledgement of him. After a beat, he inclined his head towards her and returned the smile. Dimples emerged from his cheeks. Kindness and a hint of youthful whimsy sparkled in his green eyes, and in one fell swoop, Alex's guard washed away to oblivion. A peculiar fogginess infiltrated her senses. She couldn't seem to recall why she had come out there in the first place. Feeling stupid for staring at him, she pulled her eyes away and looked to the ground. At his feet, the beagle wagged her tail and gazed up at Alex. Alex welcomed this occasion as an innocuous conversation starter. She grinned at the beagle. "Um...cute dog," she said. "Beagle...right?"

"That's right," the man said. His smile unglued her.

"Cool," Alex said. She chewed her lip and glanced at the diner door. "Uh, well," she said to the man, looking anywhere but into his alluring eyes. She offered an awkward smile and felt her cheeks flush as she reached for but missed the door handle. After an embarrassing squawk of a chuckle, she opened the door. A warm breeze smelling of greasy chicken and cheeseburgers wafted out to the frigid air. The beagle, catching a whiff, shot off like a rocket, past Alex and into the diner, her tail wagging as she snorted and sniffed. "Hey!" Alex ran after the dog, stopping at the ketchup customer's table, where the beagle had her paws up on the edge of the bench.

Alex gathered up the beagle in her arms and glanced at the ketchup customer, whose eyes were wide as she stared at the dog. "Well!" the customer said. "You're no bottle of ketchup, but I could just eat you up!"

The man walked into the diner, his face wrinkled as he approached Alex. "I am so sorry!"

"It's alright," Alex said, handing off the beagle to him. She locked eyes with him for a moment. Her knees weakened. "Um...can't blame a doggy's hungry belly!"

Mary rounded the corner. She looked at the homeless man and her nose twitched. Her eyes blazed with irritation but her smile was intact. "What's going on here? Alex...?" She leaned in close to Alex's ear again. "I thought you were going to take care of this little problem...*not bring it inside.*"

A fire burned in Alex's belly. She swallowed the snap of a retort that begged to escape her and she chewed her lip. "I—I'm sorry, I was just—"

But Alex stopped speaking and she and Mary looked over as the ketchup customer stood, gave a smart tug to her blazer, and squared her shoulders. She gestured to Alex. "This young lady was just seating my guest. He'll want a menu and a piping hot cup of coffee. And I'll need another order of fries, and more ketchup." Alex ran the tip of her tongue over her teeth as she fought a smile.

Mary's jaw twitched as this turn of events weighed on her. She cleared her throat and regained her composure.

"Oh, didn't Alex bring you a new bottle? My apologies, Ma'am, I was certain I had made it clear to her to serve you first. Had I known…."

The ketchup customer pursed her lips. "I'll have you know your employee here already brought me ketchup. I went through it already. …Hence why I need *more* of it."

Alex was sure Mary's cheeks must have ached from the smile she forced. "Of course…Alex…?" Mary said. "Get this lady more ketchup?"

Alex smiled. "…Of course." She turned on her heel.

Mary arched her brow as she stared at the homeless man. "Sir, your dog will have to wait outside." Alex stopped and looked over her shoulder at the beagle.

The homeless man looked from Mary to ketchup customer and back to Mary again. "Oh, well I…I mean I don't really need—"

"Um…" Alex said. "I…have a rope in my car…?" She shrugged and smiled as the man's eyes swiveled towards her. "You could tie her up in the alley. She'll be safe there, for a little while. I know it's not ideal, or anything, but…that way she at least won't runaway while you're eating."

The man's lips parted as he paused in thought. "I— sure," he said. His eyes lingered on Alex. Her stomach fluttered. "…Thank you," he said. "And thank you, Ma'am," he said, nodding to the ketchup customer. "Very generous of you."

A half an hour after closing, and long after the man had left, Alex slipped out the backdoor into the alley, her dinner in a grease-stained paper bag. She sighed and gazed in thought at a rainbowy oil splotch on the wet pavement. For reasons that had nothing to do with wanting her rope back, she had hoped the man would have return it to her, but he never did. She heard a whimper and looked down to see the beagle, tied to the dumpster, staring at the bag and licking her chops. "Oh my gosh!" Alex said. "Why are you still here?" Alex looked over her shoulders, looked back to the beagle, and sighed. The fog that had invaded her senses lifted, and in her mind, the gleam of kindness in the man's eyes faded to a sickening shade of depravity. Feeling like a fuel, Alex shook her head. The beagle yelped out a single bark. Alex moaned. "...*Great*."

Chapter Nine

June 18th, 2007

<u>albertcole123@courtingconnection.wuf</u>

to: me

Greta,

Your son ought to be ashamed of himself! Not coming to see you while you're injured and then lying about it…? I can't believe what he did to you! My daughter can be a pill, but she wouldn't, nor would my grandkids, ever do anything like that. I do hope you make amends with him, because you're right, as much as they drive us nuts, family is family. I also hope he is remorseful for what he's done. Did you confront him about it? I'd have let that boy have a piece of my mind! You seem like such a good person to have that happen to you. I'm sorry. And I'm sorry for your accident, but glad you seem to be on the mend.

As for my family, well…I've got something up my sleeve, as usual, something I've been working on for a few months now. Sure am having fun with it, too. I see you have a birthday coming up. Oh say, what's your mailing address?

Take care,

Al

Chapter Ten

December, 2011

Alex opened her mother's front door and gave the purple leash in her hand a gentle tug. "Come on, Beags." The beagle lunged towards the yard; Alex pulled on the leash again and walked into the house.

She was met with her mother's cheery grin. "*Alex....!* Oh, so good to see you...it's been weeks!" She nodded to the beagle. "This must be your new pal?"

Alex put on a thin smile. "Hi, Mom. Yeah, this is...uh, the beagle." She shrugged. "...*Beags*, I guess."

Mom chuckled. "I was just telling your brother, some daughters bring home a man for the holidays, but you've brought home a dog! That's almost as good, I guess!" She patted Alex's arm.

Alex dropped her eyes to one side, sighed and followed her mother down the hall and into the living room. Her brother Vince was seated on the sofa, hunched over with his arms on his knees and his giant bright blue eyes glued on the television.

"Hey, sis," Vince said. He spared a glance for the beagle. "...Find the owner?"

Alex shook her head. "...Nope. It's been a week, and nothing. I'm thinking about just keeping her. Might be nice to have a dog."

"Cool," Vince said. With a jerk of his head, he cracked his neck. "Name it yet?"

"Um, well...I've been calling her *Beags*," Alex said.

Vince tore his gaze from the screen to look at Alex. He wrinkled his brow. "That's the stupidest name I've ever heard." Alex frowned and glanced to one side.

"Are you really going to keep her, Alex?" Mom asked.

Alex shrugged. "Yeah, I mean, I paid the pet deposit, so unless her owner comes looking for her, yeah…Beags is mine." She smiled as the beagle looked up and cocked her head. "And I'm hers."

A wheezy laugh that turned into a cough sounded from down the hall. Alex arched her brow. "Grandpa's here?"

Vince rolled his eyes. "Shoulda heard him earlier. He spent ten minutes screaming at the toilet about proper dental hygiene."

Alex sent a worried frown towards the hall. *"Ten minutes…?"*

"Yup," Vince said. He grinned and wiggled his brow up and down. "Rach and I timed him."

Alex pushed out a long sigh. "He *needs* to be taking his medication…!"

Mom frowned and gave a dismissive wave. "Oh, Alex, honey…your grandfather could be drowning in a pool of bird squirt and would refuse the helping hand of God Himself!"

Vince ruffed up his spiky hair and cringed as he shook his head. "Nice, Ma …Paints a picture, really."

"Why you no good pile of rat vomit!" The beagle cocked her head towards the hall. "I'LL BEAT THE SNOT OUT OF YEH!" The leash ripped out of Alex's hand as the beagle shot down the hall and into the dining room, where Grandpa stood facing the wall, a scowl on his face. Alex and Mom hurried after. "COME OUT AND FACE ME LIKE A MAN!" Grandpa shouted.

"AROWOWOWOW!" Beags said.

Alex's eyes widened. "Beags, no! No bark!" She frowned and fell silent as Mom touched her arm and nodded to Grandpa.

Grandpa glanced at the beagle, his bushy brow sinking towards his eyes. "PUKE-BUTT YELLOW-BELLIED COWARDS! AGHH, I SEE YEH! I SEE YEH TRYIN' TA SNEAK UP ON ME!"

The beagle's nails scraped against the window sill as she rested her paws on it and craned her neck. "ARROWW! AROWOWOWWOO!"

Alex's mom snorted, clasped her hands together and shut her eyes. A wheezy squeal escaped her lips and she shook with laughter. "He, he, he…! *He's found his match!*"

Alex chuckled and shook her head. Grandpa continued to shout at no one, and Beags, her brown eyes fierce with a wild spark, shouted right along with him. Vince appeared, a question written on his face. "Is your dog….?"

Alex laughed and nodded. "Yes! …They're like two peas in a pod!"

Vince cocked one eyebrow and nodded to Grandpa, who was all smiles as the beagle licked his whiskered face. "…Rach! Get in here!" Vince said.

A tall redhead with a glass of merlot in hand appeared from the kitchen. "Whassit? …Up?" She pressed her palm to her chest and hiccupped.

"Check it---Gramps has a new best friend," Vince said, pointing to the beagle.

Smirking, Rachel strutted over to Vince and kissed his cheek. Her eyes swiveled to Alex. "Alex," she said. "I'm so happy you got a dog, Alex. *We were all starting to worry about you.*" She giggled and snaked her arm around Vince's back, hiding her face as she downed the rest of her drink.

Any form of mirth left Alex's face. Mom said something to her, but it didn't register in Alex's mind. A high-pitch tone rang its lullaby in her ears, drowning out the others in the room until they became only vague shapes and background noise. Her eyes rested on the only person who had any amount of definition. Grandpa was hunched over, scratching Beags' ears. The beagle wagged her tail, whimpered and pawed her new friend's legs.

After dinner, Alex took Beags out to potty and volunteered to do the dishes, knowing the few minutes of solitude it would grant her while everyone else retired to the living room for the football game. The hot water soothed her chilled hands as she plunged them into the filled sink.

"Hey Ma...?" Vince's voice boomed through the house.

Mom's voice rang out like a song. "...*Ye-es?*"

"The sound's all jacked up on the TV in here," Vince said. "How do you feel about watching upstairs?"

There was a pause and a dramatic sigh from Mom. "...Whatever makes you comfortable!"

Alex chewed on her lip and scraped a food bit on one of the plates with her fingernail. The ceiling groaned under footfalls upstairs. An obnoxious commercial chirped through the heating vent in the wall.

"I'm just saying," Alex heard Vince say. "...Obviously she can afford *something*—she got a dog!"

"Last year we got her a new stereo for her car," Rachel said. "She gave us a painting of a banana. ...*A banana*. And no offense, but it looked like something done by a *five year old*."

"Shhh, she's right downstairs!" Vince said. "The vents...! For God's sake Rachel, learn how to whisper!"

"She just needs gentle encouragement," Mom said. "She's fragile. ...Always has been. She might not ever be successful, but we're her family, and we're going to support her dreams. Because *that's what family does*."

Alex's felt her soul go numb. She turned off the water, dried her hands and crumbled onto a kitchen chair. She stared at the floor while pressure built behind her eyes. Tears streaked her cheeks and dripped from her chin.

The floorboards in the hall creaked. Alex made haste to wipe the tears from her face. Grandpa and Beags came in. Grandpa pushed his glasses up onto the bridge of his nose and smiled. "...Ah, there's my pretty Lexi girl."

Alex sniffed and smiled through her tear-stained face. "Hi, Grandpa. Can I...get you a cup of coffee or something?"

Grandpa frowned in thought. "No, no...." He heaved a sigh, fished his wallet out of his pants and lowered himself to the chair next to her. He opened his wallet and took out a folded bill. With a small grunt, he threw a hundred on the table.

Alex frowned at the money. "Grandpa...what's this for?"

"For you," Grandpa said. "Don't get too excited, it's not a hand-out. I expect you to work it off. My mantle is about to have an opening. Paint me something good. ...Something to inspire a story."

Alex bit her lip. "Oh, *Grandpa...*" A fresh round of tears threatened to fall, but she swallowed hard and pinched her face, determined to keep them in. She furrowed her brow. "Wait...what happened to the Van Gogh you had?"

"Ugly mess of dog squirt," Grandpa said. Alex snorted and pulled her lips inward to suppress a smirk. "I need a Lexi Rothman original to match that beautiful landscape piece in my bedroom," Grandpa continued. He grunted again and tossed another hundred on the table. Alex furrowed her brow and sighed. "Go shopping, Lex," Grandpa said. "Buy something for yourself. Pretty girl like you needs pretty things. Go to the mall. I'll watch the pup." He gave a furtive look to the hall, sighed and trained his tired eyes back to Alex. "...You have no business being around these miserable people."

A few more tears dripped down Alex's cheeks. She swallowed hard, got to her feet and hugged Grandpa's neck. "You don't have to do this. You should save your money for something important."

Grandpa patted her back. "Sweet girl," he whispered, "I *did*."

Chapter Eleven

June 20th, 2007

gretagal45@courtingconnection.wuf

to: me

Al,

My son and I are on speaking terms, but I am disheartened to say it's all very formal and lacks the warmth it used to have. My daughters and I are quite close, so, it's not all bad. And when John, my other son was alive, we were close, too. I didn't confront my other son about it, mostly because at my age, I'm tired of the drama. I've had enough of it to last a lifetime. I've dealt with some pretty dramatic characters, working as a waitress, coworkers and customers alike. I was assaulted by a customer when I was in my 30's. Nothing too bad happened, but he did get frisky with his hands and called me a derogatory name. The manager told me I was being dramatic and that it was my "job" to keep the customer happy. Grant told me to quit after that (Grant being my late husband). I stayed at home with the children and he took on a second job.

Mailing address? I do hope you're not planning to send me anything for my birthday, goodness knows I don't need a thing! You're too sweet! …But, I won't be stubborn mule about it. I'm at:

P.O Box 92A

Peony, AZ, 79046

What's your address? I'd like to send you a little something, too!

-Greta

Chapter Twelve

December, 2011

A blast of warm air greeted Alex as she pulled open the mall door. She rubbed the cold from her arms and readjusted her purse strap on her shoulder, wincing as her muscles protested with a dull cramp. She walked past what seemed an endless parade of the same clothing displays…blue jeans, red sweaters and snowflake window stickers. She bought a cinnamon roll and a latte, found a secluded table and swung her purse off her shoulder, which collided with her coffee and knocked it off the table. The lid popped off and the coffee erupted onto the floor, splattering Alex's shoes and jeans. "…*Shoot!*" Alex winced and stepped away as a sticky coffee river formed and snaked towards her. "*Darn it*, anyway!" She pressed her palm to her forehead and groaned.

"I'll take care of that, Miss." Alex turned her head to see a familiar set of kind eyes. The homeless man, though clean-shaven and hair trimmed, was still recognizable. Behind him was a clunky yellow mop bucket. He pulled a rag out of his pocket, got to his knees, and dabbed Alex's shoes.

Alex frowned. "…*You!*"

"Sorry," he said, looking up as he held the rag out to her. "Would you rather do it yourself?"

Alex gave a distracted shake of her head. "*You…*" she said again, pointing at him. "…You!"

He shrugged. "I also go by Pete."

Alex's cheeks burned and her jaw twitched. *"You abandoned your dog!"* Disgust ransacked her expression. "What kind of person *does* that?"

Pete stood up and retrieved the mop. The head splattered a bit of cleaner on her shoes when it plopped to the floor. "I went to get her," he said, nodding as he pushed the mop forward. "...After dinner. But she and I had a good long discussion. We decided it was time for her to move on...bring joy to someone else's life. She suggested, and I agreed, that the pretty waitress who was so kind to us would be the perfect candidate for a good home. And so I left her there."

Alex stared at him. She swung her purse back on her shoulder and folded her arms. "...A good home? ...*Right.* So you just...left your dog, hoping some lady you don't even *know* would take her home? What if I had taken her to a shelter? She could be *euthanized* by now!"

Pete frowned, put the mop in the wringer, and pulled the lever. "Is she?"

"Is she what...? ...*Dead?*" Alex's eyes went wide. "No! *Of course she isn't!* I wouldn't *do* that to some poor, defenseless creature!"

"So you still have her?" he said.

Alex nodded. "Yes." She pointed at him. "But I'm in *no* position to be taking in animals. When I'm not busting my butt at the diner, I'm an artist, and if you didn't know, that doesn't exactly pay well. Right now, it doesn't pay anything at all, and the way my life is going, I don't think it will ever pay anything at all, but *that's* another story entirely! Bottom line, I can't afford a dog...I just...I can't. But I'd much rather have her living with me than with someone who just *deserts* her. So I hope you don't think you're getting her back, because you're *not.*"

"You're an artist?" Pete said, plopping the mop on the floor again.

Alex frowned. "You don't even want your dog back?"

Pete shrugged. "She's not really mine. So, please, keep her. She'd do well with a good keeping." Alex crossed her arms and lifted one brow.

"You'll make money off of it...eventually," Pete said. "The art, I mean. ...Crazy, in fact, the price of some paintings, though some of it is worth every penny. I saw one the other day, in a pawn shop. They wanted two-hundred for it. It was a nice piece...simple, but lovely. It was a banana—a variation of and a nod to a famous painting, if I'm not mistaken. ...Very well done, though I'm no critic."

Alex, her stomach clenched, mustered all her energy to keep herself from crying. With her luck, she wasn't surprised that Rachel had pawned the banana painting, but it didn't make it hurt any less. She licked her lips several times and forced a smile. "So...!" she said, her voice strained with emotion. She cleared her throat and relaxed her stomach muscles. "You have a job, that's great!"

"Yeah," he said. "Mrs. Appleton was kind of enough to offer me this gig. ...Kind of her, because I don't have a physical address. She was also kind enough to list my address as her cabin up by Lake Wilderness, for the bank, so I could set up my account. ...Real wonderful person, Mrs. Appleton. Says I don't owe her a thing, and somethin' about her makes me believe it."

"Mrs. Appleton...?" Alex said.

Pete nodded. "...The generous lady who wanted ketchup."

Alex frowned in thought. "Ah...yeah...she gave you a job? That's cool. Really cool." She chewed on her lip. "Um, if you, uh...if you need a place, I hear the Alpine Complex is pretty affordable."

Pete smiled and glanced at the ground. "I appreciate you thinking of me, but I'm not looking for a place. I've got some thermal blankets now...raingear...I'm good to go."

Alex blinked and frowned. "Oh. Okay, sure...I mean...well, it's really none of my business."

Pete's brow bent into a fair arch. "There's a method to my madness." He glanced up to one side. "I find owing anyone anything...irksome." He shrugged, his lips going into a simple smile as he looked back to Alex. "Mrs. Appleton is the exception. She's not the type to give with expectation for it to be reciprocated. She gives freely, and when she gives, it's with a blind eye and a good heart. He stared into the distance, his eyes gaining a glossy veneer. "But, really...I'm better off on the streets," he said, returning the mop to the bucket. "Trust my word on that."

Alex nodded. "Sure...that's cool." She arched her brow, crossed her arms and in spite of herself, smirked. "Although...well, let's see here. Other than being a *dog-abandoner*, I don't know enough about you *to* trust your word."

"Yeah, I was...hoping we might change that," Pete said. His eyes darted back and forth and he looked as though a load of words had gotten tangled in his mouth. He licked his teeth and cleared his throat. "...Meaning I'd love to take you out to dinner tomorrow night."

Alex arched her brow. "You're asking me out...?"

The apples of Pete's cheeks turned pink and he swallowed hard. "I, uh...yes...?"

"I…don't think so," Alex said. "Sorry…."

"Why?" he asked. "Ah, you don't want to go out with a homeless man? Is that it?"

Alex felt heat consume her face. She shook her head. "No, that's not it at all! I don't want to go out with someone I just met, *and* with someone who abandons dogs."

Pete smirked. "You're not going to let that one go easily, are you?" He shoved his hands into his pockets and sighed. "I apologize, Alex. I didn't mean to offend you. I didn't see it as abandonment. Like I said, she wasn't even my dog…just my temporary business partner, but I don't suppose that makes it any better for you."

A sardonic chuckle flew from Alex's lips. "*Right.* So, hmm, you used her to make money, then left her? …*Tied up*, even?" She rolled her eyes. "Oh, yeah, you sound like a real upstanding guy to me. Totally change my opinion of you now."

"Good," Pete said, a gentle grin on his face. "So, you'll reconsider my invitation for a date?"

"Not even a little bit," Alex said.

Pete gave a thin smile and shook his head. "…The beagle," he said, clasping his hand around the mop stick. "She's looking for something. I saw it in her eyes, first time I saw her….they were…I don't know, *restless*…longing and lonesome, like nothing in the world was quite right, and wouldn't be until she found it. And what she's looking for, well, it wasn't me. It might not even be you. Don't be surprised if one day she ups and leaves you."

"You mean like what you did to her?" Alex said.

Pete gave a thin smile. "Funny." He shrugged. "It's just...I thought you'd of all people would understand what I mean."

Alex furrowed her brow. "Okay...why do you say that?"

Pete scratched his nose and sniffed. "I see the same look...in *your* eyes." Alex frowned. "That date is a standing invitation," he said.

"Still don't know you," Alex said.

"Well, this is our second meeting," he said, wheeling the mop bucket around to his right side. "How many meetings will it take for you to consider me someone you know?"

"I don't know...third, I guess," Alex said. "...But it can't be here, that doesn't count."

Pete's dimples appeared again. "Third meeting?"

Alex nodded. "Third, and then...I'll *consider* it."

Pete's brow shot upwards. "How kind of you. You just better hope I'm not already taken by then. "Alex suppressed a smirk. "So," Pete said, "what did you name the beagle?"

Alex gave a self-depreciative chuckle and rolled her eyes. "...Beags. I named her Beags. Stupid name, I know."

Pete shook her head. "Not at all. ...Suits her, in fact. Oh, uh...here," he said, reaching into the pocket of his uniform. He pulled out a crinkled envelope. He fished out a ten dollar bill and handed it to her. "...To replace the latte."

Alex shook her head. "Oh, no...it's okay," she said, giving a dismissive wave.

"Please," Pete said. "I insist…it's on me. Or rather, it's on a generous fifteen-year-old boy."

Alex snorted a laugh and pointed to her shoes, still blemished with splattered coffee. "…Better than on *me*, I guess, huh?"

Pete pulled his lips inward and licked them, shaking his head. "Wow…that was bad. *Really* bad."

A grin tugged at Alex's mouth. "It's, uh…it's been fun chatting with you, Pete."

Pete rolled the mop bucket a few paces behind him and smiled at her, locking his eyes with hers. "See you at the third."

Alex turned to leave, and judging by the weightless feel in her step, the fog had returned. It swirled its tendrils around her mind, coaxing her into the delightful chaos from whence it came. She strode out into the cold, a stupefied smile on her face.

Back at her parents' house, Grandpa was waiting on the porch, plopped in a wicker chair with his bushy brow aimed at his lap.

"Grandpa…?" Alex said, frowning as she touched his arm. "What's wrong?"

"Oh, Lexi," he said, looking up at her, his eyes shining with tears. "I'm so sorry…I don't know how she got away from me…!" Alex's stomach went to knots. His voice sounded so distraught, so helpless and lost. "… Took her out so she could do her business, and bam!" Grandpa continued. "She took off! Should'a known it, too, confound it! …Her being a hound, and all. I'll put up reward signs! We'll find her! I'm sure she'll show up at the shelter, and when she does, I'll take her back home to you, first thing!"

"Oh, no! …She got *loose*?" Alex's eyes darted up and down the street. She sighed and looked back to Grandpa. Humiliation plagued his face, but the thought that he could ever do anything to disappoint Alex was laughable. "Grandpa," Alex said, a gentleness to her tone, "*it's okay.*"

Grandpa frowned. "What'ya *mean*, it's okay?"

Alex shrugged. "She's probably just looking for something…." She paused in thought. "…Something she's not going to find with me. I mean, if nothing else, she'll find her way back to her proper owner."

"Could be," Grandpa said. He scratched the top of his head and furrowed his brow. "In fact, you're probably right about that one. She'll likely be just fine. And…if all goes well, I mean…" He gave a deep shrug. Alex thought she saw a glint of mirth in his eyes. "…You just might see her again."

"I hope so," Alex said.

Grandpa glanced up at her in his periphery. "So…how was the mall? Find anything…interesting? Anything…*catch your eye*?"

Alex's lips twitched. She fingered the ten-dollar bill in her pocket. "We'll see."

Chapter Thirteen

December 18th, 2007

December 18th, 2007

albertcole123@courtingconnection.wuf

to: me

Greta,

I've done a dreadful thing and I'm not sorry.

I pulled the biggest scam of my lifetime on my family, even little Lexi. I haven't decided if I'm going to tell her yet or not, the thing that I did, but I will tell you this. What I did involves an old pill bottle, sugar, and a good amount of acting. Just got so dang tired of my family acting like fools, thinking they know what's best for me when the lot of them don't even come to visit me! Lexi, well, she's wonderful, but I know that sweet little girl couldn't keep a poker face, so I chose not to let her in on my fun. I can't keep up the charade forever, so I guess eventually I'll have to come clean.

I'll be sure to tell you the details of my misdeed when you come to visit. What time does your flight arrive, again?

Al

Chapter Fourteen

December, 2011

Mom tossed her car keys to Aaron. "You need practice driving on ice," she said.

Aaron furrowed his brow and shook his head. "Uh, I *know* how to drive on ice."

"Good!" Mom said, pushing out a puff of white breath into the cold air. "You can prove it to me this morning by driving your little sister to school. No practice, no license." Aaron mumbled something under his breath and slid into the driver's seat. Mom's lips went into a thin line as she got into the passenger side.

Hannah climbed into the back and buckled her seatbelt. She unbuckled it again, letting it retract at a slow pace and pulled downwards again, clicking it once again. Without looking up at her mom, she said, "Aaron has a lot of emotions. He shouldn't be driving. I saw a movie where a driver was distracted by too many emotions. She got in a wreck because she wasn't paying attention to the road. We got in a wreck, once. A drunk driver hit us. Our car was totaled. My seatbelt wasn't buckled all the way because I was wearing a big winter coat. I thought I heard it click, but my brain was fooled. I got a concussion. Now I make sure my seatbelt is buckled, every time. I don't want another concussion. If Aaron gets into a wreck, I could get another concussion."

Aaron turned his head and scowled at Hannah. "We're not gonna get in a wreck." He turned over the engine.

Hannah shivered as a blast of frigid air from the vent above her blew down on her head. "You can't know that," she said, as Mom adjusted the knobs on the heater. "There is no way for you to know that for sure."

Mom pushed out an agitated sigh. "Okay, so we'll...put on some Christmas music. Nothing like a little Jingle Bells to ease the tension." She turned on the radio. An operatic *Joy to the World* sounded and Aaron pulled out of the driveway.

Hannah pressed her mitten-clad palms over her eyes, but lowered them when Mom spoke. "So...guys, I have something to tell you," she said.

"I'm not a guy," Hannah said. "I'm a girl."

"Of course you are, Hannah....I'm...sorry," Mom said.

Aaron rolled his eyes. "Tell us what?" A pregnant pause incited a crease to Aaron's forehead. He stared at her. "...*Mom*?"

Mom sighed and glanced back at Hannah through the visor mirror. "So...the deal fell through on a project in Barlow. Now, nothing's changed as far as Christmas is concerned, but....it means we're not moving, not yet anyway, because we can't afford the land where we wanted to build our new house. So, for now, we're staying put."

Aaron glanced at Mom in his periphery and frowned. "That sucks, Mom. I'm sorry. I know you were looking forward to it."

"Well, yeah," Mom said. "But...that's life, I guess."

"That's strange," Hannah said.

Mom looked over her shoulder to Hannah. "What's strange?"

"We're not moving," Hannah said, "…But…you don't look *sad*."

Mom shrugged. "I *am* sad, Hannah. But…you know, I'll get over it."

"But it's what you *wanted*, Mom," Hannah said. "You should be sad. When you don't get what you want, the feeling you get is sadness. You show sadness by crying or frowning….or shouting."

Aaron gave a grim smile. "Well you see, *Hannah*, some people just know how to actually *control* their emotions, while other people only know how to act like a spoiled brat."

Hannah frowned and Mom glared at Aaron. "My point is," she said, looking back to Hannah, "you don't always get exactly what you want. Life doesn't work that way. I'm just happy so long as we have a roof over our heads, and we do, so…it's time to be thankful, even though yes, I am sad."

The three Davenports fell silent, each lost in their own thoughts. Aaron picked up the speed as they pulled out onto a main drag, but slowed again as a semi joined the ranks ahead of him. The driver of a zippy little car behind the trunk declared his impatience as he blared his horn. Aaron frowned and sighed. "This song sucks," he said, winding down the volume on the radio to zero.

"I liked it," Hannah said. "Turn it back on! Turn it back on, Aaron! I liked it! *I liked that song!*"

"You're not the one driving," Aaron said. "So your opinion doesn't count." Traffic moved again, but Aaron came to a stop at the next intersection to permit a woman on a motorized travel scooter to cross the road.

Hannah scowled. "You're not being fair, Aaron. Mom always lets us listen to music when she drives!"

"Aaron," Mom said. "Turn it back on, you can keep it low volume."

"No!" Aaron said. "I shouldn't have to cater to her stupid little demands. I'm the driver, and if I have to listen to that racket, it will distract me." He drove through the intersection and turned the heat down to low.

"*I'm cold*!" Hannah said. "Turn the heater back up, Aaron!" She thrust her fists into her seat. "Turn it back up *right now*!"

"No!" Aaron said. "I'm sweating bullets up here! And shut up, already, *gah*, you're obnoxious!"

Mom sighed and shook her head. "Okay…pull over."

Aaron's features melted into a putrid scowl. "*Why*?"

"Well clearly your sister was right," Mom said. "I don't know what your problem is, but if anything, it's your attitude that will distract you, not the music. Pull over."

"Mom, I'm fine!" Aaron said.

"Aaron, I said *pull over*," Mom said.

Movement caught Hannah's eye as a dog darted out into the crosswalk. Her stomach went to knots. "AARON…!" she shouted.

"I see it!" Aaron said. The tired screeched as he slammed on the brakes. The car jolted to a halt, Mom's hand sliced through the air and collided with Aaron's chest. The dog darted into the right-hand lane and a driver there honked their horn.

Aaron gripped the steering wheel and swallowed hard. Mom's staggered breaths slowed, she dropped her hand from Aaron and the car to their right whispered along the wet pavement. "Hannah...are you okay?" Mom asked. "Is everyone okay...Aaron?"

Aaron nodded and rolled the tension from his shoulders. "I'm okay."

Hannah didn't answer, but scanned the road ahead, now seeing no sign of the dog. "Where did the dog go?" A *meep* of a horn sounded twice from behind them.

Mom's sigh was tinged with irritability as she gestured to a parking lot. "Pull in there, out of the way, Aaron!"

"Okay, okay!" Aaron said, his hands rigid as he pulled into the lot. He shifted to park and Hannah jumped out of the car.

"Hannah, wait!" Mom said. Hannah darted across the intersection. Mom hurried to catch up with her. The dog, stationed by a street light, broke away from a good sniff on the sidewalk and took in the scent of Hannah's shoes. She squeaked a yawn, wagged her tail and with a lolling tongue, jumped up and pressed her paws into Hannah's thighs. Hannah's insides froze and her head reeled It was as though for a moment, all the rest of the world was made up of only dogs, and every one of them wanted to eat her for breakfast. Her breath caught in her throat. She stepped back. The dog's paws slid back to the ground.

Mom slowed her jog as she reached Hannah. "You can't just run off like that into the street, Hannah! What if a car had hit you?"

Hannah shrugged. "I looked both ways. There weren't any cars. I have fast eyes. ...Because I have a fast brain."

Mom sighed and diverted her attention to the dog, who sat on the sidewalk, her hind legs comically sprawled out on each of her sides. "Well, isn't she just darling? She seems to be okay, too." She crouched and rubbed the dog's ears. "No tag...no collar...are you homeless, Sweetheart? Looks like a beagle...."

"We need to take it to a shelter," Hannah said. "That's what you're supposed to do. We can't leave it out in the cold. It could freeze and die, or it might get hit by a car. Those are serious dangers. We need to help the dog. That's what you're supposed to do."

Mom nodded and scooped the beagle into her arms. "Yep, you're right, Hannah. I'll drop her off at the shelter before I head to the office."

They returned to the car, Mom with her arms full of beagle. Aaron wrinkled his forehead as Mom unloaded her cargo to the backseat. Hannah gave the dog a hesitant frown, angling her body away from it.

The beagle's tail whipped back and forth as she leaped onto the center console and sniffed Aaron's neck and arm. Aaron chuckled and ruffled the dog's ears. "Hey, cool, a beagle! Stay out of the road, you goof! I almost pancaked you, you know!" The beagle pressed her wet nose into Aaron's neck. "Um...?" Aaron said, looking to his mom. "So what, are we keeping her?"

"I'll take it to the shelter after I drop you two off at school," Mom said.

Satisfied with Aaron, the beagle changed directive and pressed her paws to the door opposite of Hannah, licking the condensation on the windows.

"I'll need a late note, Mom!" Hannah said. "They won't let me into class if I don't have a note from a parent!"

"Yup, gotcha covered," Mom said. "...Aaron, out of the driver's seat. *I'm* driving." She gave Hannah a covert look and dropped her voice as she glared at Aaron. "You and driving need to take a little break from each other. If you think acting like you did back there is going to earn you a license next month, you are sadly mistaken, Buddy. When I tell you to pull over, *you pull over*."

Aaron rolled his eyes. "Whatever...*Jeeze*...." He unbuckled, mumbled more unintelligible words, and got into the passenger seat. Mom's jaw twitched and Hannah saw a fire in them as she glared at Aaron and got into the driver's seat. The beagle, having finished the window, angled herself towards Hannah and eyed the other window.

Hannah, with the pace of a cat stalking its prey, inched her fingers towards the beagle's nose. She jumped and shot her brow upwards as the beagle bathed Hannah's fingertips in kisses. Hannah screeched and Mom jumped and gasped, but the screeching turned into fits of laughter as Hannah got used to the sensation. Every impact of the beagle's wet, warm against her skin sent a fresh jolt of surprise through her. "Oh gosh, oh gosh, oh gosh!" Hannah said. "What a funny dog! Do my fingers taste good? Mom, the dog thinks my fingers are popsicles! Do you think she likes popsicles? Oh gosh, oh gosh...! *Mom!*" Mom smirked and exchanged glances with Aaron, who, in spite of himself, managed a half-smile.

But Hannah frowned in confusion as the beagle turned circles. She grew quiet and rigid as the dog crawled onto her and curled up into a ball on her lap. Hannah held her breath and not sure what to do with them, angled her bent arms to the sides, but soon the feeling of the warm body snuggled against her incited a small smile on her face. Through the visor mirror, Mom surveyed the interaction. The beagle's eyes darted upwards towards Hannah's face and gleamed with longing. Hannah couldn't pull her own eyes away from sight. A whimsical emotion crept into her mind and like a dose of oil, loosed her stiffened muscles.

She lowered her arms, placed one over the top of the beagle's tan head, and stroked her fur with delicate hesitance. The beagle sighed and nuzzled Hannah's hand. Sheer joy struck Hannah's face. "*It likes me!*" she said. "Mom, the beagle *likes* me!"

Mom turned and smiled. "Yeah," she said. "She sure does."

Chapter Fifteen

December 19th, 2007

gretagal45@courtingconnection.wuf

to: me

Al,

There's been a little problem with the flight. I'm so embarrassed, but the funds I thought I had fell through. I did a little investigating and found out my son has my bank account info. He took my money, claiming he needed it to pay a bill and thought I wouldn't mind. Says he can pay me back soon but he's never paid me back for loans in the past. I'm frustrated but I know if he's in need I couldn't stand the thought of him struggling. You probably think I'm a pushover. I just don't have the heart to tell him he can't keep it.

I can start saving again. It might take me four or five months but I can and will save up enough money to come and finally meet you!

Brokenhearted,

Greta

December 20th, 2007

albertcole123@courtingconnection.wuf

to: me

Greta,

I know it's none of my business, but I really think your son is taking advantage of you. Anyway, maybe *I* can come and see *you*? Or, if you want, I can wire you the money so we can continue with our original plan. You can pay me back whenever. I'm willing to do what it takes to make this work. I do hope we can still meet in person, even if it's not for a few months yet.

Chapter Sixteen

"Excuse me...sorry!" the female half of the teenage couple said. Alex darted out of the way of the couple, who were all but walking on top of each other as they strolled past Alex in the mall. The girl craned her neck to look back at Alex, almost tripping on her boyfriend's feet. She laughed, righted her gait, and grinned at Alex. "Sorry!" she said again. Her face was tinged with the glow of infatuation as she beamed at her boyfriend. He chortled and offered a sheepish grin to Alex, who smiled their pardon. The couple turned back around and stuck their hands in each other's back pockets. Like pieces of a puzzle, their young, flawless bodies seemed to click together into perfect place. Alex tucked her hair behind her ears, smoothed out her faded t-shirt and gave an upward tug to her jeans. With a cleansing, self-assuring sigh, she slipped into the restroom. She checked for feet in the stalls, and seeing none, she turned to face the mirror.

She released a breath she had been holding. "Okay...okay, you can do this," she said. "Heya, Pete. I know we said that here didn't count, but...surely we can make an exception? I mean, if you're still interested...." A pout met her lips as she shook her head. "God, that sounds so *stupid*!"

A toilet flushed and heat rushed to Alex's cheeks. She kept quiet as her fellow bathroom patron exited her stall. Alex caught a glimpse of her in the mirror. She was a young girl, and didn't look at Alex as she washed her hands.

"Don't worry," the girl said. Alex sucked in a short breath and arched her brow. She frowned and glanced from side to side, unsure if the girl had been addressing her, as she hadn't been looking at Alex when she spoke. The girl turned off the faucet with a paper towel, grabbed another paper towel and dried her hands. Here, she spared a glance for Alex. "I talk to myself all the time," she said. "It's not weird. It just means you're smart."

Alex laughed, a little louder than she had anticipated. "Um…okay, sure," she said. "That's one way to think about it, I guess. …Thanks." With a downward gaze, the little girl left, and soon after, her head held high with as much confidence as she could muster, so did Alex. She went to the food court, sat and waited, but there was no sign of Pete. She walked the mall, keeping her eyes peeled, but after an hour, she pushed out a heavy sigh and left the mall.

Chapter Seventeen

December, 2011

Hannah woke to a wet nose on her neck. Groaning, she opened her eyes and turned on her lamp. The beagle locked eyes with her and whimpered. A shiny red tag, emblazoned with the name *Lynx* and Mom's phone number, hanged from the beagle's collar and jingled like a Christmas bell as Lynx itched her ear. Hannah rubbed the sleep from her eyes and sat upright. "Gotta do your doggy business, Lynx?" She rolled out of bed, pulled the sheet and blankets taut, smoothed them over, and slid her feet into her slippers.

The beagle dug her nose into Hannah's laundry hamper and snorted and sniffed. Hannah frowned. "...*Again*? What is so interesting about my laundry pile, huh?" She slipped her finger under the beagle's collar and tugged her away from the hamper. "No, Lynx. I told you already. I don't want beagle boogers all over my dirty clothes." But the beagle lunged back towards the hamper. Squinting, Hannah looked to her clothes pile. She sucked in a sharp breath through her nose when she saw her jeans. "Oh!" she said. She pulled out a charred, faded green dog tag from her jeans' pocket. "Is this what you're smelling?" She held out the tag in her open palm. "Lynx, is this tag *yours*?" The dog took in a hearty sniff and wagged her tail.

Hannah opened her bedroom door and the beagle zipped to the front door. "Hold on, hold on...." After frowning and fumbling with the metal hook, Hannah at last attached the leash and opened the door. The beagle shot out into the night, slipping away from the ill-attached leash. She sniffed the frozen ground in staccato snorts and scurried down the sidewalk like a bolt of lightning, further away from Hannah. "Hey!" Hannah shouted. "You can't leave! You're *our* beagle now! We adopted you! That means you stay with us forever!" Hannah sprinted down the sidewalk after Lynx, but after the fourth block, she lost sight of her. She sprinted back to her apartment and as Mom was gone for the night for work, she burst into her brother's bedroom. "AARON!"

He shot upright and gasped. "Wha...? Hannah...? What's wrong?"

"*Lynx ran away*!" Hannah said. "I took her out so she could go pee in the grass because she's a dog and can't use the toilet like humans do, and the leash wasn't attached because it was poorly designed and she *got loose*! I tried to catch her but she's so fast! But I think I know where she's going, so if we hurry we can beat her there!"

Aaron dug his face into his pillow and gave a dismissive wave. His sleep-addled voice rumbled and croaked. "We can look for her tomorrow, and after Mom gets back she can help look. Go back to bed."

"But she might get ran over before then!" Hannah said. "Or she might freeze and die! Or someone might kidnap her and sell her to a research lab! *They do bad things to dogs in research labs, Aaron!* Those are serious dangers! Please, Aaron! Aaron, please, we have to go! We have to, we have to go now, we have to go now, we have to...!" She paced his bedroom floor and dug her fingers with a great force into her hair. "*Aaron, we have to go now!*" She stamped the ground with her foot and turned on Aaron's light. *"NOW!"* GET UP *NOW*, AARON!

Aaron inhaled, held his breath for a count of five, and exhaled a steady, slow breath through Hannah's tirade. He sat up and squinted at her as the light assaulted his vision. "Alright, shut up already! Screaming at me won't bring her back any sooner! And if you want my help, you better *stop*." Hannah quieted herself but fidgeted and twiddled her thumbs. "Okay...Hannah...look...the dog's long gone for now," Aaron said. He put up his hands in a gentle manner. "The buses stopped running hours ago, and we're not going to catch her on foot."

"But you can *drive*!" Hannah said. "Mom leaves her spare key on the rack in the kitchen! Come on, you've driven her car by yourself before! ...*Remember?*"

Aaron cringed. "Uh, yeah, I remember. That was a stupid dare from my *stupid* friends when I was a *stupid* thirteen-year-old, and I shouldn't have done it. And I'm not doing it now, either! I don't have a *license*, Hannah!"

"Aaron...*please!*" Hannah said, biting her lip as tears came to her eyes. "I love her so much and I don't want to lose her! Please...please...we have to go now...we have to...please! I never ask you to do anything for me! But I can't drive because I can't see over the steering wheel! *I need you!* You're my older brother! You're supposed to help me and right now I need help!"

Aaron sighed, plunged his arms to his side in defeat, and stared up at his ceiling. "Okay." He threw back his covers and shook his head. "Mom is going to kill me."

Hannah, with tears streaking her cheeks, lunged towards Aaron and threw her arms around his neck. "*Thank you!*"

Aaron froze in surprise as he glanced down at Hannah. His muscles went lax and with a chuckle, he patted her back and gently tore her away from him. "Get your coat."

Minutes later they were in the car. Aaron buckled his seatbelt and Hannah buckled and unbuckled hers, then buckled it again. Aaron stared at the steering wheel and shook his head. "So where's this alleged place?"

Hannah frowned. "It isn't alleged. It's a real place. You meant to say Lynx is *allegedly* there."

"Okay, whatever," Aaron said. "…Still no clue where it is."

"I know where it is," Hannah said. "I'll tell you how to get there." She cast him a frantic look. "Hurry up, we're wasting time!" Aaron sighed and started the engine.

Sometime later, they left the city limits and drove into a wooded area. Houses were sparse and with all the turns Hannah directed, the roads became more and more unfamiliar to Aaron. He arched his brow. "You think Lynx came out this way?"

"Yes," Hannah said. "Turn left up here."

Aaron sighed. "You're sure you're not just getting us *lost*?"

"I'm sure," Hannah said. "Just keep driving."

The forest whispered an eerie stillness, making the SUV's xenon headlights seem like an unruly intrusive house guest. Majestic evergreens towered over them, the frosted bottommost boughs of which twinkled with a wintry glow.

They drove onto a short bridge and down a hill. Near the bottom, the car fishtailed. Hannah held her breath and squared her shoulders against the back of her seat as Aaron pumped the brakes. As they slid at a snail's pace a few feet, Aaron pressed a shielding hand against Hannah's sternum. They came to a stop. Aaron pushed out a shaky breath. "Whoa…." he said. He looked at his sister and retracted his hand. "You okay?"

Hannah nodded. "Yes." She frowned. "You put your hand across me like Mom does. Why?"

Aaron wrinkled his brow and shrugged. "I don't know. Because Mom does it, I guess. It's instinct or something."

"But that doesn't make any sense." Hannah said. "That's what seatbelts are for."

Aaron sighed and thrust his hands through his hair. "I don't know, Hannah. It just…happens, okay? A kneejerk reaction." Hannah frowned in thought while Aaron craned his neck, looking at the icy road ahead of them. "I knew this was a bad idea…soon as we can, we're turning around and going home."

"But we're almost there!" Hannah said. "And we came all this way! We can't go back, not yet! We *can't*!"

Aaron groaned and glanced at her. "We're almost there? How close?"

"It's less than a quarter of a mile, if that!" Hannah said.

Aaron's cheeks puffed out as he exhaled. "Okay." He inched the car onward. His knuckles whitened as he death-gripped the wheel.

"You're a good driver, Aaron," Hannah said. "You can drive on ice really well. If I didn't know it would get you into trouble, I would tell Mom so. I'd tell her your hand flew out across me, too. I think she'd like that you did that. Then she'd know you're a good driver."

Aaron frowned. "*Don't* distract me."

"Okay," Hannah said. She grew quiet and gazed out her window again. *Jingle Bells* came on the radio but was stifled as Hannah gave a wary side-glance to her brother and cranked the radio's volume to zero. A few moments later, she pointed to the right. "Turn up there."

Aaron sighed. "Hannah, we've been driving forever. I'm not even sure my phone can find a satellite to get us back home. Are you sure we're almost there?"

"Don't worry," Hannah said. "I can get us back home. And anyway, that's it up there. No more turns after this one." She glanced at him. "...We're here."

Aaron scanned the illuminated roadway and spotted the turn in question. "Okay...." A crease to his forehead, he made the turn, into what appeared to be an overgrown empty lot. Gravel popped under the tires and intermittent patches of tall, yellow grass gave way to them. Aaron stopped as the headlights illuminated a stone structure. The bottom of it was squat, rectangular and covered in a mess of dried branches and rotten leaves. Between the dying foliage, Aaron could see the shadowed hollow of an opening in the center, and a tower of corroded bricks, wrapped in holly and ivy, stood on top of it. "Huh...cool," Aaron said. "...An old fireplace."

Hannah unbuckled her seatbelt. "Come on!" She leaped out of the car.

"Hannah, wait!" Aaron said. Grumbling, he turned off the car, kept the headlights on, and hurried to catch up with his sister.

"*There she is!*" Hannah said, pointing to the stone structure. Lynx was curled up on the hearth, behind a mess of branches and ivy, her face tucked into her belly. Hannah crept up towards her. Lynx lifted her head and peered up at Hannah.

Aaron, not seeing the beagle at first, craned his neck and leaned to one side until he saw her white-dipped tail. "Oh yeah," he said. "Heh...you know, she looks pretty comfortable for sleeping on an old pile of bricks." Hannah cast him a wary glance as he scooped Lynx up into his arms. Lynx angled her head up at Aaron and groaned.

Aaron frowned. "She's soaking wet."

"She took the shortest distance," Hannah said, "which means through the creeks."

"Better get her in the car before she turns into an icicle," Aaron said. He furrowed his brow. "I wonder why she came here?" His frown deepened as he looked at his sister. "And how did *you* know she'd *be* here?"

"Easy," Hannah said. "Because it's her home."

"Uh…okay…*right*," Aaron said. He frowned down at and patted the beagle's belly, which was more bulbous and tight than he had remembered. "Jeeze, I didn't know how *fat* she's gotten 'til just now. I told you that you were feeding her too much." Lynx yawned, rubbed her wet, cold nose into Aaron's forearm and wiggled as he carried her back to the SUV. Hannah followed along behind them. "Okay, Lynx," Aaron said. "Time to go back home, you little escape artist." Hannah opened the door and Aaron plopped the beagle onto the back seat.

Hannah shut the door and frowned at Aaron. "I said this *is* her home. You can't take her home, because she's *already* home."

Aaron's brow went to wrinkles. "What do you mean?"

"This used to be her home," Hannah said. "…Before it burnt down." She dug into her pocket and pulled out the tag. "This was Lynx's," she said. Aaron frowned and took the tag from her. "She sniffed it and came straight here." Hannah said. "I found the tag here, yesterday."

Aaron opened his mouth, shut it again and frowned. "Wait, wait, *wait*...yesterday? You were here *yesterday*? How did you manage that one?"

"Field trip," Hannah said.

"I thought you were visiting a farm, or something," Aaron said.

"We did," Hannah said. "We passed this place on the way. I saw the chimney and was interested. So when everyone was having lunch, I walked back here. I found the tag by the fireplace. I didn't think anything of it until Lynx smelled it."

Aaron stared at her. "...By *yourself*? Hannah! Wow! That's...." He shook his head. "You shouldn't have done that! You can't just wander off like that on your own!"

"I know I'm not *allowed* to do it," Hannah said. "But I'm *capable* of doing things like that safely, so I don't see the point in having a rule against it."

Aaron threw his hands up to the air and shook his head. "Oh...*oh-ho*! ...If Mom ever finds out...!"

Hannah frowned. "Are you going to tell her?"

Aaron's shoulders sank and he frowned. "Well...no...." He rolled his eyes. "Because she'd find some way to blame *me*, I'm sure."

"I doubt that," Hannah said. "You weren't on my field trip. How could you possibly be at fault?"

Aaron gave a thin, dour smile and plunged his cold-nipped hands into his pockets. "Well, anyway," he said, "I won't tell Mom." Sincerity stole into his eyes and graced his smile as he shrugged. "I mean, the fact that you managed to sneak away like that without any teachers or other kids finding out…I don't know, it's pretty impressive."

"It wasn't difficult," Hannah said.

Aaron rubbed his thumb over the worn surface of the tag. "Too bad the name's rubbed off, huh?"

Hannah stared up at him. "Why?"

Aaron shrugged. "It'd be cool to know what her actual name is—or was."

"Her name is Lynx," Hannah said.

A small smirk played on Aaron's lips. "Yeah…you're right. Her name is Lynx." He sighed and leaned up against the side of the SUV.

Hannah sniffed and looked at the sky. "It's going to snow."

Aaron shifted his gaze upwards. "Eh, I don't think so. It's cloudy, but it's been way too dry."

"I smell it," Hannah said, still looking to the heavens. "There is an increase in the odor of nitrogen dioxide, formaldehyde, nitric acid and sulphate. They all have distinct odors. Lynx probably smells them, too."

Aaron arched his brow. "Uh, *right*, what *doesn't* that dog smell? She's all nose. And you really think *you* can smell all that stuff?" He frowned and shook his head. "You're just listing things you read in a book. You can't actually tell that it's going to snow just by how it smells."

Hannah continued to peer into the cloudy darkness above them. Aaron fumbled with the keys and started for the driver's side door, but he stopped and looked up when Hannah lifted her hand and pointed. Aaron frowned and followed her finger's directive, angling his head towards the heavens again. Marvel rendered his mouth agog as a tiny, single snowflake descended. Time seemed to hold its breath in awe as more flakes peppered the air. Aaron shook his head and grinned at his sister. "You truly are remarkable, Hannah."

Hannah dug her hands into her jacket pockets and shivered. "We should go home now. The road conditions won't get any better with snow."

Aaron shrugged. "Eh…let's stay a while. Go get Lynx. Just make sure her leash is attached this time."

Hannah pushed out a heavy sigh, but did as Aaron requested. She attached the leash, frowned in thought, unattached the leash and attached it again. She tested it with a small tug before letting the beagle out of the car. Lynx panted and lunged towards the grass, moving her body in quick arches and making Hannah stomp with each step to keep herself from falling. A spark of crazy ignited in the beagle's eyes. She ran in circles around Hannah, disturbing the small amount of snow that had accumulated on the ground. Hannah cracked a smile. "I think she likes it!"

Aaron grinned. "*Yeah*, she does! Heh…that dog's meant for winter, I think."

"She's meant for *Christmas*," Hannah said. "She's our family's Christmas *present*."

Aaron chuckled and nodded. "Yeah… a beagle for Christmas. …*The Christmas Beagle*."

Hannah smiled in thought. "*The Christmas Beagle*…that's you, Lynx!"

Aaron looked at Hannah. "You really like her, don't you?" With a zestful gleam in her eyes, Hannah nodded.

Aaron laughed and pointed at Lynx, who was now rolling from side to side in the snow and pawing at the air with a silly grin on her face. "Look at her! She's going nuts! I guess everyone loves snow." He looked upwards in thought, a broad grin on his face. "You know what I used to do when I was a kid?"

"What?" Hannah asked.

"*This*," Aaron said, falling to the ground. He spread his hands and feet, moving them like windshield wipers. "Snow angels," he said. "Eh, not really enough snow yet, but enough for somewhat of an imprint. Try it, Hannah."

Hannah blanched, narrowed her eyes and shook her head "It's cold...and *dirty*! The only reason I would ever lie on the ground is to look at the stars, and *only* on top of a blanket, but...there's a cloud cover."

Aaron sighed. "Here," he said. He took off his jacket, laid it on the ground next to him, and gave it a pat. "...Compromise. At least sit down, so I'm not the only idiot freezing my butt off down here." Hannah twiddled her thumbs glanced to one side. Her motions stiff, she lowered herself to the jacket, taking care to not let any part of her touch the ground. Aaron took Lynx's leash and the beagle took every inch of slack afforded to her. Hannah drew her knees to her chest and crinkled her nose as a snowflake kissed the tip of it.

Aaron pulled his body taut and gave a contented, rumbling yawn, shaking as the cold crept up through his shirt to the small of his back. He gazed upwards again. The flakes grew fatter and scrambled the air in a frenzy of white. "So..." he said, turning his head, "Little sister...what do *you* want for Christmas?"

"Astronomy books," Hannah said.

Aaron laughed. "Uh, yeah, you say that every year. You have enough to fill a library already…isn't there anything *else* you want?" He grinned and arched his brow. "…Might just have to get you the stars themselves this year."

Hannah frowned, tugging on the leash as Lynx pulled away from her. "That doesn't make any sense. Unless you're going to have a star named after me, but Mom already did that two years ago. I don't want another star named after me."

"Yeah," Aaron said. He blinked as a few flakes tickled his lashes. "Guess I'll have to figure something else out."

Hannah pulled her lips to one side and looked at her brother.

Aaron frowned. "What?"

"Do you remember that pinewood derby car you built for me, when I was six?" she said. "I was really scared to go down the hills, but I wanted to win first prize…a space helmet."

Aaron chuckled. "Yeah, that cheap, tacky thing. You know, I could have made you a better space helmet myself."

Hannah glanced to one side. "I thought it was cool."

"Okay," Aaron said. "So, what…*that's* what you want for Christmas? …A space helmet? …Or another racer?"

"No," Hannah said. Her top teeth dug into her bottom lip as she deliberated for a moment. "I just…I remember being really scared of crashing," she said. "I didn't want to go fast. But you reminded me that real scientists have to be brave, especially astronauts. That…if they aren't willing to take risks, there won't be a reward. You told me it was okay to be scared, just so long as I didn't let it keep me from doing what I want to do." A tiny smile twitched in her lips as she looked at the ground. "And you said I *am* a real scientist, and because of that, it meant that my brain was wired *to* be brave."

Aaron smiled. "Heh, yeah…I remember. You came in second place, but you were awesome." He pivoted his head and looked upwards at her from where he lay on the ground. "What made you bring that up?"

Hannah twiddled her thumbs and shrugged. "I don't know." She looked at him. "Thanks for helping me get Lynx back."

"Yup," Aaron said.

Silence fell between them as they watched the falling flakes blanket the fireplace. Lynx sniffed her way over to Aaron, turned several circles, and plopped down next to his hip. Aaron draped his arm over her. With each passing second a thicker thread of tranquility wove itself into the night. The seconds blurred together as a moment, and the moment, flecked with falling snow, stretched out into infinity.

Hannah glanced at the snowy tall grass in her periphery. "Aaron," she said, looking back to him, "I think I know what to get Mom for Christmas."

Chapter Eighteen

December 21st, 2007

gretagal45@courtingconnection.wuf

to: me

Al,

With the hospital bills, I think it would be better to just put off us meeting. Times are tough for a lot of people, and I'm not excluded. I am deeply sorry…I was so looking forward to meeting you.

Love always,

Greta

December, 2011

"*Aaron…?* " Mom's voice echoed from the hall as Hannah poured herself a bowl of cereal the next morning. "You wouldn't happen to know anything about the gas gauge on my car being empty, would you…? I *know* it was full when I left!" Lynx cocked her head and looked up at Hannah, whose stomach went to knots. She sat down at the kitchen table and pushed the holly berry centerpiece a smidge to the left, making it in her eyes, more centered. Though they had made sure to clean up the SUV's interior after the wet beagle, refilling the car with gas had slipped their minds.

"Yeah, um…" Aaron said. "There was sort of an emergency last night. My friends' car broke down out in the country and they needed a ride. I didn't think you'd mind."

There was a beat of silence. Hannah moved the centerpiece back towards the right. *"Are you kidding me?"* Mom said. *"Again…? Really? Aaron Thomas Davenport*...! What were you *thinking*? And tell me this, why couldn't their parents give them a ride?"

"I…don't know…?" Aaron said. Hannah sighed. She could hear the weakness in his tone. This was a battle he would lose.

"…*I don't know*?" Mom said. "Well let me tell you what *I* don't know! With your obviously poor judgment skills, *I* don't know if I can trust you to watch Hannah this weekend without taking off in another joyride! This is a huge client for me, Aaron! But I guess I have no choice but to stay home, which puts us out even more. We'll be stuck in this apartment for the rest of our lives…is that what you want?"

"I don't really care!" Aaron shouted. "Either way, I'll be miserable, so it really doesn't make a difference to me where we live! You're the one who wants to move, not us! You know Hannah doesn't want to leave, but you don't care what she thinks! You just do whatever you want and expect us to go along with it! And fine by me if I don't have to watch that brat, because if *she* does anything wrong, guess who gets the blame for it? *Me!*"

"*That's a load of bull!*" Mom said. "This doesn't have *anything* to do with Hannah!"

"Yes it does!" Aaron shouted. "Don't you get it? *Everything* has to do with her, you're just too blind to see it! *You* get frustrated with her fixations and you take it out on me! It's like...you can't control her, so you focus on me, instead, because hey, I'm the easy kid, right? I'm easier to control! Well I'm getting really tired of it! I'm not Hannah, so if you have a problem with her, take it out on her, not me!"

"*Excuse me?*" Mom said. "*You're* the one in trouble here, and *you're* the one trying to put the blame on Hannah! *You* took the car, Aaron...without a license, for the second time! Unless you're trying to tell me your *eleven-year-old* sister is to blame?"

"Nope," Aaron said, a formidable tightness to his tone. "Once again, she's perfectly innocent. ...Wouldn't dare to accuse precious Hannah of anything. She might throw a tantrum, and then we'd really be in for it, wouldn't we? I mean *wow*, Mom, God forbid you actually parent your own child." Hannah moved the centerpiece towards the bay window, away from her. She tapped the sharp tip of one of the leaves with her pointer finger, and pushed the centerpiece towards the left again.

"You don't get to speak to me like that!" Mom shouted. And *you know what...?* I've had enough of this!

I've given you a lot of slack lately, and now I'm regretting it! You can say goodbye to getting your license next month, *and* you can say goodbye to your social life! *You're grounded*! I can't even tell you for how long!"

"Oh yeah, for *what…*?" Aaron asked. "…For taking the car? …Or for calling you out on your *oh-so excellent parenting skills*?"

"Phone," Mom said. Hannah heard the sound of her mom snapping her fingers. "Hand it over. …No screens, no friends…*nothing*."

Hannah rotated the centerpiece a hair clockwise, then counterclockwise. Her stomach felt like a rock. Avoiding the creaking spots on the floor, she slinked out of the kitchen, taking care to be quiet as she shut her bedroom door behind her.

Chapter Nineteen

December 22nd, 2007

albertcole123@courtingconnection.wuf

to: me

Greta,

Thought it over and I'm wiring you some money. It ought to be enough to cover some of your bills, your round-trip flight, and maybe some nice new things for yourself. You're a pretty lady, and pretty ladies should have pretty things.

Love Always,

Al

December, 2011

That evening, while Aaron sulked in his room, Hannah held out a printed paper over the holly berry centerpiece. Mom fished out her reading glasses from her purse and took the paper. "What's this?"

"Land for sale," Hannah said. "The bank wants to get rid of it, so it's super cheap."

Mom frowned and scanned the details. "...A fireplace and chimney...left after house fire...heh. You know I think I've heard of this place. ...Never considered it for a project site, though." She peered over the paper at Hannah. "Worth checking out, I guess."

"I want this land," Hannah said. "I want to build our house on this land."

Mom scrunched her lips to one side. "Oh yeah...? Why's that?" Her brow lifted with a note of humor. "And why the sudden change of heart? I thought you *loathed* the idea of moving?"

Hannah stared at the table. "I just think it would...be a good place to build our house."

"Well," Mom said, "like I said...I mean, we can look *into* it...."

Hannah chewed her lip. "I have to tell you something."

"Oh, yeah...?" Mom said. "What's that?"

"The other night when Aaron took the car, I went with him," Hannah said. "His friends didn't need a ride. That's not why he took the car. He took it because I asked him to do it. Lynx got loose. I knew where she went because I found this," she said, digging into her pocket.

She pulled out the tag and handed it to her mother, who frowned and lifted the mangled piece of metal up to the light. "I walked to the property," Hannah said, "last week...during the field trip to the museum."

Mom's eyes went wide and lowered her arm, letting the dog tag slip from her hand to the table. "You *what...?*" Hannah took in a deep breath, locked eyes with her mother and nodded. "You wandered away from the group? ...From the *chaperones?*"

"It wasn't that far," Hannah said. "I know it was breaking the rules, but I saw the chimney, and I wanted to investigate. It looked so interesting, just a chimney, standing in a big empty lot. I found the dog tag there and put it in my pocket. I walked back to the farm without anyone knowing where I had gone. When I got home, I read about it online...the house fire. There was no mention of them owning a dog, and I think that's because the dog wasn't there at the time of the fire. I *think* the dog they owned was an *escape artist*, like *most* dogs of her breed. I dug deeper and did a search for the family, and after a lot of dead ends, I found *this*," she said, reaching into her pocket again. She pulled out a folded-up printer-paper photo, and showed Mom. Mom's brow arched as she took the photo from Hannah. "That's the family," Hannah said. "...The mom, dad, and their little boy. ...The Rosewoods. They all died in the fire. Look, there...in the corner. You can see a dog's tail and part of a foot, and the boy is holding onto a leash, but looks like he's about to fall over, because the dog is pulling on the leash!"

Mom nodded. "Yeah, I see it."

Hannah wrinkled her face and sighed. "...The tag, Mom! Don't you get it...? Lynx caught a scent on the tag, and she ran off. We found her at what used to be that house, by the only part of the house that didn't burn down! And that's how I know!"

Mom frowned. "Know *what*…?"

"Lynx used to live in the house, before it burned down!" Hannah said. "She was the Rosewood's dog! The tail in the picture…? It matches hers! You can't see what her name used to be, though, on the tag, but I *know* it's hers. When Aaron and I got to where her house used to be, she was all curled up, by the fireplace. She looked like…like…." Hannah scrunched her face as she struggled to find the right word.

"…Like she was *home*." Hannah looked up to see Aaron standing in the doorway. "It's weird, Mom," Aaron said, "but I think Hannah's right."

Mom turned and arched her brow at him. "…So, you lied to me?"

Aaron shrugged. "Yeah…"

"Yeah, but…" Mom said. An incredulous stupor overtook her face as she gestured towards Hannah. "You lied for *her*!"

Aaron shrugged again and stuffed his hands into his pockets. "She's a worthy cause, I guess." A small smile crept onto Hannah's lips.

Mom shook her head and smirked. "…Never would have thought it in a thousand years." She sent Aaron a sharp look. "You're still grounded…and *you*," she said, pointing at Hannah. "You're in for it too, young lady. You can't just wander off by yourself, especially not on a school trip! You could have ended up suspended! …Or worse, *kidnapped*!"

"I know," Hannah said.

Mom sighed and looked at the paper again. "I guess…we'll talk about it later." She glanced around the floor. "Where's the runaway, hmm?" She whistled, and Lynx trotted in from the next room. She plopped her chin on Mom's lap, making her eyes go big as she stared up at the human. Mom chuckled and leaned down to give Lynx a good scratch. She frowned and lingered on the beagle's belly, pressing her palms to it and to her sides. "Oh…" Mom said. "Oh…*oh my*…definitely didn't notice this before!"

Aaron shook his head and frowned. "What…?"

"Um, well," Mom said, her lips thin and forehead wrinkled as she looked to Hannah. "Lynx is pregnant."

Chapter Twenty

December 22nd, 2007

gretagal45@courtingconnection.wuf

to: me

Al,

Oh, you are too generous! I couldn't possibly accept, but I know you, and I know you'll be unhappy if I don't accept. But, it can't be a gift…I fully intend to pay you back, just as soon as I can. You're a wonderful man, Albert. I can't wait to meet you!

Love,

Greta

December 22nd, 2007

albertcole123@courtingconnection.wuf

to: me

Greta,

Sure thing, Sweetheart! I will send the money today. I can't wait to meet you!

Al

Chapter Twenty-One

December, 2011

Let it Snow pleaded its case on the TV's holiday music station but freezing rain still pelted the living room window. Hannah turned up the music and caught a faint whiff of cinnamon from the clay gingerbread men as she popped the lid off the fat gray ornament tub. She sat down on the edge of the sofa, peered at the ornaments and smiled. Thanks to the dividers she had made years ago, each ornament was in its rightful dwelling, every snowman with his kin, every Santa mingling with the other Santas, and each individual glass reindeer enclosed in bubble wrap and snuggled together. From the top right section, Hannah's favorite dark blue wooden stars, accented with glitter, twinkled their greetings to her. She looked at her mom, who stood by the tree with a fistful of stringed lights. "Everything looks to be in order and intact," Hannah said.

"Great!" Mom said.

Behind Hannah, fast asleep, Lynx thumped her tail against a stiff throw pillow. Hannah peered at the beagle over her shoulder. "Look, Mom, even Lynx is excited for her new house! She's *dreaming* about it!'

Aaron reached around the tree to take the string of lights from Mom, glanced at Lynx and chuckled. Mom looked over her shoulder and grinned at Lynx. "Oh, yeah! Isn't that precious!"

"Yes, it is," Hannah said. "Imagine how disappointed she'll be if she doesn't get her new house *right away*."

"Hannah," Mom said, "We've been *through* this."

"It's for Lynx!" Hannah said. "She needs her new home…please! Can't we at least start? She's going to have her puppies soon! She needs a safe place! She needs her house! What if she runs away again? Next time she might get ran over by a car! She needs a new home for Christmas! She needs it! She needs us to do this! We have to do it, we have to do it, we have to do it…! *We have to…!*"

Mom shook her head, taking the lights back from Aaron. "No, Sweetheart! I haven't even seen the place yet! And in case you forgot, there's still the little matter of the loan! One thing at a time!"

"You don't need a loan!" Hannah said, frowning in concentration as she straightened the wire hanger on a cloth snowman. "We have money in savings!"

"Hey, *Davenport Industries* isn't doing as well as it used to," Mom said. "That savings account has dwindled down over the years. We can barely afford materials for the house, much less the land itself! No. A loan is a must, and it is a must to wait for it to *be approved*."

"It's out in the country," Hannah said, looking upwards in a dreamy gaze. "The stars will be so much easier to see. It's perfect for an astronomer!" She put the snowman back in its section and picked up a blue star.

Aaron rolled his eyes as he tugged at a small section of the lights that had re-tangled. "I don't know, Hannah." He gestured toward the tree. "You won't even let us have a real tree. How are you going to deal with living in a forest?"

Hannah frowned. "I don't mind real trees that are outside, where real trees *belong*. Fake trees don't drop pine needles all over the floor and they don't make my head hurt while I'm trying to do my homework."

"Oh come on!" Aaron said. "You're not even allergic. You just don't like the smell, and it isn't even that strong."

Hannah glowered at him. "Is, too."

Mom sighed. "Aaron brings up a good point, Hannah. You've been there twice. But living out there will be a different story. Are you sure you're really are okay with this? I mean…having a house at this place will make you happy?"

Hannah bounced to her feet and nodded. "Yes! Aaron likes it too, right Aaron?"

Mom laughed. "Since when do you care what Aaron thinks?"

"Well, he has to live there, too!" Hannah said. "We had a lot of fun there, didn't we Aaron? It snowed on us, and we made snow angels, and Aaron gave me his coat!"

Mom lifted her brow. "…This place sounds like it performs miracles, to get the two of you getting along. You're certain you'd be happy out there, too, Aaron?"

Aaron shrugged and gave the string of lights a tug, righting it where it lay on the branches. "Like I said, it's alright, yeah," he said. "I mean, aside from it being kind of creepy that people *died* there…" He chuckled and shrugged again. "I can tell Hannah really likes it." He looked over at Lynx as she stretched and slinked off the couch like a slug. "I think Lynx likes it most of all, though." He narrowed his eyes and gave a weak smile, craning his neck to look around the tree at Mom. "…But first sign of a ghost…? Nope. I'm out."

"There's no such thing as ghosts!" Hannah said. "If you see anything that you think is a ghost, it's only a figment of your imagination."

"Yeah, yeah," Aaron said. "Like I said, the place is nice."

Mom gave a curt nod. "Alright, then. I'll call the bank first thing tomorrow. I can't promise anything, but let's just see if we can rush this process along." Hannah beamed and hanged the blue star just left of dead center on the tree.

Chapter Twenty-Two

December 26th, 2007

albertcole123@courtingconnection.wuf

to: me

Greta,

How was your Christmas? Did you get the gift I sent? Did you receive the funds alright? I didn't hear from you the last couple of days, just wanted to make sure all is well. Look forward to meeting you.

Love,

Al

December, 2011

Aaron peered out the window, watching as Hannah climbed into her friend's mother's car. Lynx, tail wagging, pressed her paws against the window frame and whimpered. "Aw," Aaron said, scratching her ribs. He rubbed her belly and gave a low whistle. "Boy, you're ready to pop, aren't ya? Don't worry…your girl will be back." He got to his feet and checked his pants for his wallet. "…And so will I." Lynx peered up at him with a gloss of question in her brown eyes. "You can keep a secret, right?" Aaron said. He smiled and opened the door. "Stay here, Lynx. I'll bring you back a treat, I promise. Just don't tell Mom." He cringed. "I'm kinda not allowed to leave the house." Lynx sat and licked her chops. Aaron smiled and sighed. "Alright, fine…you can come."

Minutes later he climbed out of a banged-up van at the house construction site. Two other boys emerged as well; all three of them carried wooden beams on their shoulders. Aaron tightened his grip on a bucket of power tools. From inside the van, Lynx cocked her head and pressed her paws up against the window.

"Where exactly do you want this stuff?" one of the boys asked Aaron. He looked to the rough frame of a house that surrounded the fireplace, but Aaron shook his head.

"Keep walkin'," Aaron said. "I'll let you know when to stop."

"Uh…Aaron?" the other boy said, nodding to a man just ahead as he appeared from behind a wooden beam.

"Oh…uh…I think I know who that is," Aaron said. Frowning, he approached the man.

The familiar homeless man pointed at Aaron and smiled. "...*Truck man!*"

"Yeah," Aaron said with a smile. "What brings you here?"

"Read about this place in the paper," he said. "Even though it's far from town, it has the potential for a good temporary home," he said. "But...it seems I'm too late," he said, as he gestured to the house frame.

"Heh, yeah," Aaron said. A sheepish expression fell over his face. "Um, my uh...my family is building a house here."

"Ah," the man said. "I see. Glad this land is being put to good use. Hey, let me know if you need any help...I have experience in construction.

Aaron chewed his lip. "Actually...I really could use some help with...something. Something else I'm working on. It's just...well I can't really *pay* you...."

"Yeah," Colin, one of Aaron's friends said, "he's not paying us, either." Aaron rolled his eyes.

The man put up his hand and smiled. "I don't mind. It'll give me something to do when I'm not at work."

"Alright," Aaron said. "Well...there are a few more things in the van. ...Tools and materials."

"Lead the way," the man said.

Colin unlocked the van and Lynx leaped out onto the ground. "Agh, no! Ugh, Aaron, the dog--!"

"Lynx, NO!" Aaron shouted.

Lynx booked it right into the homeless man's arms. He crouched, chuckled and permitted her to bathe his face in kisses. "...Missed you, too!" he said.

Aaron frowned. "Um…you know Lynx?"

"*Lynx*, huh?" the man said. He rubbed the beagle's coat in a vigorous manner and nodded. "We're old friends, yes."

He felt Lynx's stomach and shot an amused look up at Aaron. "Well, truck man, when we last spoke, you said your family didn't want any pets. Now it seems you're about to be blessed with a whole family of them."

Chapter Twenty-Three

January 2nd, 2008

albertcole123@courtingconnection.wuf

to: me

Greta,

I hope everything is alright. It's not like you to not respond. I hope to hear from you soon, Sweetheart. I really am looking forward to meeting you. Don't think I've ever wanted anything more, for a long time.

-Al

December, 2011

"She's gone…she's gone *again*!" Hannah's voice rang out through the apartment. "We have to go to the house now, Mom! We have go leave, we have to go, we have to!" She thrust her mother's purse and keys into her hands.

Mom sighed. "Breath, Hannah…take a beat. We're going to the house anyway, so if that's where Lynx is, we can get her back. Don't worry, it'll be okay."

"*You can't know that!*" Hannah said.

Aaron came down the stairs and frowned at Hannah. "What's up?"

"Lynx is GONE!" Hannah screamed, her face going white.

Aaron sighed. "…*Again*? Ugh…!"

"We'll find her…come on!" Mom said.

Hannah, after bucking, unbuckling and buckling her seatbelt again, drew her feet up onto the seat, chewed her nails and muttered to herself while Mom drove

. When they arrived at their destination, the moment Mom parked the car, Hannah flew out her door and ran to the unfinished house. Mom and Aaron jogged to catch up with her. She circled the fireplace and shook her head. "*She 's not here*! What if she had her puppies? They could be hurt!"

Aaron frowned. "…Be right back," he said, before darting off towards the woods.

"Aaron!" Mom shouted. "Where are you going?" Without turning back around, Aaron offered her a lazy wave and broke into a jog.

A noise coming from behind Hannah and Mom turned their heads. A scruffy looking man was staring at the house frame, tapping his chin. Seeing that it wasn't Lynx, Hannah groaned and tugged on Mom's arm, urging her to continue the search elsewhere.

Mom grabbed Hannah's shoulders in a protective manner and frowned at the man. "Can I help you?"

"…Sorry, Ma'am," the man said. "Just, was wondering if you could use a helping hand."

"Mom!" Hannah said. "Let me go! Come on, we need to find Lynx! *Mom*…!"

Mom ignored Hannah and gave the man a hesitant smile. "Well, that's awfully nice of you, Sir, but…well I think we have it handled. Thank you, though, just the same."

"Sure," the man said. "But I do have some experience in construction. My, uh…my apartment gets a bit lonely. Looking for a hobby to pass the time. Since I'm not expecting payment, I do hope you'll put me to work."

Mom's mouth twitched and she was about to respond when Aaron returned, puffing and red-cheeked. He gave a hesitant frown. "Oh, uh…hey, Pete."

Mom shot a glare at Aaron. "Aaron, where in the world did you run off to? I'd appreciate it if you'd stop just disappearing whenever you please!" She frowned. "…Wait, you know this, uh, *gentleman*…Aaron?"

Aaron smiled at the man. "I've, um…seen him around, yeah." He looked at Hannah. "I have something to show you," Aaron said, then his eyes swiveled to Mom. "Just trust me on something for a minute, Mom, please. I have something I want to show Hannah. We'll be back soon, I promise."

Mom crossed her arms and pushed out a heavy sigh. "Fine, just…hurry up, please."

"*Did you find Lynx?*" Hannah said.

Aaron grinned. "Come on!" He latched onto Hannah's hand and though she wore a hesitant frown, he led her into the forest.

"Aaron, where are we going?" Hannah asked. "Do you know where Lynx is? I don't like it when you don't answer me right away! This is *important!*"

Aaron chuckled. "Just come on!"

Hannah saw it while they were still a good distance away from it. Through the trees, there was a clearing, where stood the beginnings of a lofty structure. "What is that? Where did it come from?"

"It's an observatory," Aaron said. "Well, it's not finished yet, but the bare bones are there." He shrugged. "I built it."

They quickened their pace, Hannah with her eyes glued to the observatory the whole time. When they arrived at their destination, she gawked at her brother. A rare note of awe struck her tone. "*You built this? …For me?*"

Aaron nodded. "Well, I had some help. Come on…check it out!"

A thoughtful frown on her face, Hannah followed her brother up the stairs to the top of the tower. Hannah dropped her jaw and gasped. In the corner, peeking out from under a pile of wool blankets by the window was Lynx's white-dipped tail. "Lynx…?" Hannah said. The beagle's head emerged from the blankets and she nosed the blanket off of her. Hannah broke into a broad grin. Lined up at Lynx's middle were four newborn beagle puppies.

Hannah, chewing on her lip, took slow strides toward Lynx. "You're a *momma*, Lynx!" she said, crouching as she observed the family from a distance.

"All healthy, too, I think," Aaron said from behind her.

Hannah craned her neck and glanced at her brother. A crease met her brow. "You knew she'd be here...didn't you?"

Aaron shrugged. "I had a hunch. She's tagged along here and there. Pete—that guy back there—he's the one who brought the blankets for her, so she could hang out with us while we worked...though this is really the first time she's used them, I think."

Hannah smiled. "You did a good job, Aaron. Lynx is comfortable here. She considers this part of her home, too."

"Yeah," Aaron said. "I've been thinking about that...you know the picture of the Rosewoods and Lynx...? Well, she's pulling away in that photo, which I thought was strange, because now that her family is gone, she's been pulling *towards* the house...towards them, almost, as though she's waiting for them to come home. It's like...she realized what she had, but only after it was gone. That's why I did this for you. You drive me nuts sometimes, but, you know...you're my little sister." He shrugged and dug his fingers into his pockets.

Hannah got to her feet and hugged him, tighter than he had anticipated. "You're the best big brother in the whole entire universe," she said. Aaron chuckled and returned the embrace.

Chapter Twenty-Four

March 5th, 2008

albertcole123@courtingconnection.wuf

to: me

Greta,

It's been three months since I last heard from you. I'm thinking about contacting the police, because I am truly worried something horrible has happened to you. Maybe you're busy. I don't mean to be a bother, it's just not like you to not respond. I really like you, Greta. You've been a fresh breath of air in my stale life. I'm not a religious man but I've been praying all is well.

Love,

Al

April 2nd, 2008

gretagal45@courtingconnection.wuf

to: me

Al,

This is hard for me to do. If you haven't already, you'll find the money was wired back to you this morning. I have something to confess. I'm not a widower. I'm not even a woman. For many years, I was a scam artist. I say was, because I've decided to stop. I haven't been arrested, yet, but after our correspondence I expect that will change. All I can offer you, other than your money back, is my sincere apology.

-Ashamed

March 28th, 2008

albertcole123@courtingconnection.wuf

to: me

I see. What made you decide to stop?

Al

April 30th, 2008

gretagal45@courtingconnection.wuf

to: me

Al,

I…saw something. I legally can't talk about it, not until the trial is over. But what I saw changed me. All I know now is big changes are coming my way. I'm not sure what that means, yet, but…it's coming.   I suppose you can know one thing…my real name. It's Pete.

May 2nd, 2008

albertcole123@courtingconnection.wuf

to: me

Pete,

I won't be calling the police. You'll find the money was wired back to you this morning. Call it your grace fund. Use it well.

Al

May 7th, 2008

gretagal45@courtingconnection.wuf

to: me

Al,

I don't understand…?

Pete

May 9th, 2008

albertcole123@courtingconnection.wuf

to: me

Pete,

Let me tell you about forgiveness, because throughout my life I've seen both sides. I've learned what it means to hold on to the bitter poison of a grudge. It tears you apart, to look at the world through glasses tinted with hate and fear.

I've also learned what it means to cause immeasurable pain in others and dealing with the ache of guilt afterwards.

Now, you could be extremely gifted at scamming to the point where you use your heart-felt confession in order to get even more money out of me, but whether you've truly stopped scamming or not makes no difference to me. You've given me the opportunity to do something uncommon, something that goes against what most men would do, and for that, I thank you.

Al

May 9th, 2008

gretagal45@courtingconnection.wuf

to: me

Al,

I just don't understand it. How can you give me the money back when I confessed to you what I am? What I've done…?

Pete

May 9th, 2008

albertcole123@courtingconnection.wuf

to: me

Pete,

The secret is to never let your grace supply run low, even for the idiots of this world, but don't be a doormat, either. This is accomplished by administering said grace with both your heart and your brain. I cheated on Linda…just once, when I was away on business. It killed me, every day, knowing what I had done. On her deathbed, I confessed. It was the hardest thing I've ever had to do, but I couldn't let her leave this world without knowing the truth. She deserved better than that. So I told her. She cried, and it tore me apart, seeing my dying wife hurting, both physically and emotionally. I asked if she could ever forgive me. She lifted her frail, cold hand, touched my face and said…"always". That, my boy, is grace. It's meeting people where they are. Linda forgave me, and shortly after, I learned how to forgive myself…something I don't think I could have done so easily if she hadn't forgiven me first. Linda gave me a wonderful gift, and I can never repay her. But that's kind of the point.

-Al

May 10th, 2008

gretagal45@courtingconnection.wuf

to: me

Al,

Linda sounds like she was indeed a classy lady. I guess since you've been honest about your past, it's time for me to offer more honesty about mine. I've started browsing online support groups for former criminals. Haven't signed up for anything, just browsing for info, because I know if I say too much I'll get busted. Several people have suggested telling the story of how you ended up in crime as a form of moving on. So, I'll tell you, because right now, you're the only person I can trust, Al. Years ago I owned a small construction company. A woman named Emily Davenport came to town, put me out of business. I didn't stand a chance. She took all my clients. I lost my house. …Spent a few months on the street, saw some really ugly times. I started to mug innocent people. From there, I got back on top, got an apartment, switched to scamming people online. I hate what I've done and I hate what I've become.

-Pete

August 2nd, 2009

gretagal45@courtingconnection.wuf

to: me

Al,

As you know, the trial concluded yesterday. By now I'm sure you know the specifics, or at least the specifics according to the media. I can talk about what happened, now. I'm not sure you want to know, but it's been weighing on me, and as my only friend these days other than you is a wandering beagle, I really want to let you know my take on things. I'll copy and paste what I wrote for my own personal records:

What I went through changed me...forever. I witnessed a murder. I was half-drunk, walking home from the bar after New Year's. Several other bar patrons were in the vicinity. A homeless man emerged from an alley and approached a woman, asking for money. The woman obliged and started digging through her purse. The homeless man reached his hand out to the woman's shoulder... she had some confetti or something, from the festivities. One of the bar patrons shouted "HEY! Get away from her!" The homeless man jumped back several feet, looked so confused, so alarmed. The other man, the bar patron, he ...took out a handgun, and shot the homeless man, right there, in the chest...fell to the ground. ...People screamed...everything was a blur. It was...the most god-awful, horrendous thing I've ever seen. He died within minutes.

You might not hear from me for a while, Al. I'm making some big changes in my life and won't always have internet access.

-Pete

Chapter Twenty-Five

September 3rd, 2010

goodolboy531@courtingconnection.wuf

to: me

Ninja Flower,

Allow me to introduce myself. My name is Al. I also live in Oregon. I have a daughter, grandson, granddaughter-in-law, and a granddaughter. In my spare time (when I'm not getting into trouble), I collect art, volunteer at the animal shelter and write romance novels.

Your profile doesn't say much, but I see you like animals. I love animals of all kinds but I have a soft spot for dogs. Hope to hear from you soon.

Al

December 1st, 2011

gretagal45@courtingconnection.wuf

to: me

Al,

I met Lexi today. I was too nervous. I waited with the beagle in the alley, thinking I'd wait until Lexi got off work and talk to her then, but I got scared and left…leaving the beagle behind, thinking that it would give me an excuse to find Lexi and talk to her again. It was a stupid idea, I don't know what made me think of it. And I don't know, Al. Not sure she'd be into…you know, my type.   In other news, I've at long last accepted a job. My boss is a good person. …Didn't feel right rejecting the job offer. I think it'll be good for me.

Pete

September 9th, 2010

ninjaflower5000@courtingconnection.wuf

to: me

Al,

Well, don't you sound like the whole package!
Yes, I love animals, and as far as everything else there is to
know about me…? Well, it comes in doses, some larger
than others, Sweetie. You can't pin me down as any one
thing and my tastes are always changing. What's constant
is my passion---for people and for life. At 71 I'm still
going strong, running several of my own businesses and
loving every minute of it. I've been looking for a nice man
to balance me out, but one who can keep up with me when
I get a burr up my butt and decide to turn the world upside
down! Do you live in Geraldine? I'd love to get together
soon for a cup of coffee, my treat.

You have a knack for trouble, oh so I infer from
your reference. Good. I like my men that way. ;-)

Stay fierce, Al.

Ninja Flower

September 10th, 2010

goodolboy531@courtingconnection.wuf

to: me

Ninja Flower,

I live close by, and I appreciate the invitation, but I prefer to take things a bit more slowly, for now. I was recently a victim of a scam artist, and although that situation has been remedied, I've learned to be more wary of what I agree to online. I do hope you can understand. Hoo, boy…! You seem like a woman who knows what she wants…I like that. You're unlike any other woman I've met. I can tell you're a strong, passionate person. I'm very interested in getting to know you better.

Take care,

Al

September 13th, 2010

ninjaflower5000@courtingconnection.wuf

to: me

Al,

Oh, Sweetie! I'm so sorry for your experience! I understand, really I do. You can't be too careful these days. I just hope what happened to you didn't kill your spirit, but clearly it hasn't entirely as you had the courage to contact me. We can keep our correspondence strictly online. You mentioned you have grandchildren? None of those for me... while I've dated, I never did marry or have any kids. I'll be honest---after conquering the world, I'm ready to finally settle down, but am perfectly alright with not rushing things with you, Al. I am just so ecstatic to learn that you live in my area! The last man I dated online lived in Florida! I've caught your eye, hmm? If you're not careful, I might just catch your heart, too. ;-)

Stay fierce, Al

Ninja Flower

September 15th, 2010

goodolboy531@courtingconnection.wuf

to: me

Miss Flower,

I'm not so certain I'm ready to settle down again, but if I met the right woman…well, I suppose I'll cross that bridge when I come to it, eh? What kind of business do you run? I was a lawyer for many years.

Al

January 5th, 2011

ninjaflower5000@courtingconnection.wuf

to: me

Al,

The angel brooch you sent me is beautiful, thank you! I meant to thank you earlier, but I told you how hectic things can be for me at Christmastime. I'm glad you enjoyed the sweater! I saw it and just thought…that is SO Albert! Oh, honey, these past few months have been some of the best months of my life! Tell me, how's Lexi? That painting of hers you showed me is just divine! Tell that gal to stop wasting her time and pursue her dream, already! I agree, she's underselling herself. Worse mistake a woman can make! Give me a week with that girl…I'll whip her into shape!

I had a dream about you last night. We were dancing…holding each other so tight. I think of you, every day, Al. I do wish you'd reconsider what we talked about.

Stay fierce, Al

Ninja Flower

April 10th, 2010

goodolboy531@courtingconnection.wuf

to: me

Miss Flower,

I've been thinking about what we talked about. How about a compromise? Do you believe in fate? If you and I are meant to meet, we will. Living in the same town, it's bound to happen eventually, don't you think?

I think of you every day, too. You're the first thing I think of in the morning, and the last thing I think about when I go to bed. I look forward to your messages.

Love,

Al

April 10th, 2010

ninjaflower5000@courtingconnection.wuf

to: me

Al,

    I believe in taking the bull by the horns. Fate, like life, is what you make it.   I like you a lot, Al. I like your close relationship with your sweet granddaughter, Lexi. I love that you help homeless animals find families. I love your wacky, mock-curmudgeon sense of humor. I love, love, love your writing! I mean that, honey. *Shadowed Love* is the best romance I've read in a long while! And you're a hoot! No one has ever made me laugh the way you do. You're kind, generous and I would love nothing more than to be your gal, live, in person. I want to hug you…to kiss you, Al. I want to take you dancing! I want to memorize the way your forehead wrinkles when you're flabbergasted by the idiocy of the younger generation. I think it'd be a rotten shame if our relationship never extends outside the computer. But I will respect your boundaries. If we are meant to meet, perhaps, indeed, we shall. Hey. You keep calling me "Miss Flower". Don't you dare forget, I'm just as much Ninja as I am Flower!

    Stay fierce, Al

    Ninja Flower

April 13th, 2010

goodolboy531@courtingconnection.wuf

to: me

Miss NINJA Flower,

I'll have you know my forehead doesn't wrinkle. It merely cringes in reaction to the idiocy you referenced. Oh darling, the way you talk…I want all that, too. You're a breath of fresh air for this tired old coot. You're pure sunshine and you deserve the world. You deserve to have someone to hug, to kiss…to go dancing with you. And a go-geter gal like you, well, I'm no fool…I know you won't stick around for long if I don't make an effort. I don't want to lose you. I think we could have something really good going here. Give me time. A few months, maybe…and we can revisit the topic. Don't forget, I'll be calling you tonight. I can't wait to hear that sassy, yet angelic voice of yours.

Al

December 1st, 2011

goodolboy531@courtingconnection.wuf

to: me

Pete,

You took a vow of poverty. You're a philanthropist. Trust me, you're Lexi's type. Congrats on the job.

Al

December 3rd, 2011

gretagal45@courtingconnection.wuf

to: me

Al,

I figured out what I'm getting for you for Christmas. I've been wondering…did you ever tell your family the truth about your "mental defects"?

Pete

December 4th, 2011

albertcole123@courtingconnection.wuf

to: me

Pete,

I had a few more good shows, but I didn't keep it up for long before telling them the truth. My daughter still thinks I'm off my rocker, my grandson thought it was hilarious, his wife thought and still thinks I'm an insensitive ne'er-do-well, and Lexi, though she was hurt at first, has been able to laugh it off and makes jokes about it now. All in all, they've been very gracious with me. ...More than I expected them to be, but they're still a bunch of idiots (excluding Lexi). Eh, take what you can get, right? Don't waste your time buying me a gift. I can't imagine you'd be able to find anything this old man doesn't already have. Keep a look out for Lexi. She'll be coming your way soon.

Al

December 10th, 2011

gretagal45@courtingconnection.wuf

to: me

Al,

Sorry it took so long for me to reply. Your Christmas gift is something I already promised to you and it's high time you've received it. Not so sure I made the best impression with Alex, but she tentatively said yes to a date. Gotta tell you, I'm not sure how long we can keep our history a secret from her. She'll eventually find out that you set us up.

-Pete

December 11th, 2011

albertcole123@courtingconnection.wuf

to: me

Pete,

You're right. Let me know when you've told her.

Al

December 12th, 2011

ninjaflower5000@courtingconnection.wuf

to: me

Al,

My day was beautiful, thank you for asking! The decorators did a lovely job on my windows this year. The house just *sparkles* Christmas! I loved our conversation last night. I still think it's too funny that you call me Ninja Flower on the phone, too! I don't believe there was anything more beautiful than to hear those magical words from you, but Al, I'll be honest, and you know me, I almost always am. I want to meet you. You've found every reason in the world not to do it. I love you, and I'd like to believe you really do love me, but so long as you're not willing to meet me, I don't know that I can believe you. Turn me into a believer, Al.

Stay fierce,

Ninja Flower

December 14th,2011

goodolboy531@courtingconnection.wuf

to: me

I do love you, and I mean that. We've been dating for a long time now and I'm head over heels, darlin'. I think part of what has kept me from meeting you is...I'm afraid to hurt you. I don't want to hurt you like I hurt Linda. I don't trust myself to not do that, and I can't...I can't let myself do that, not to you.

Love you always,

Albert

December 15th, 2011

ninjaflower5000@courtingconnection.wuf

to: me

By not taking a chance you are hurting me, Al, more than you know. Give us a chance. You won't cheat on me. I'm far too fabulous to let that happen, and you're far too wonderful. I trust you, Al. I trust you. Trust yourself.

Stay fierce,

Ninja Flower

Chapter Twenty-Six

December 20th, 2011

At the sound of tires on gravel, Emily propped the back door back against the wall and walked around to the front of the house. Aaron and Hannah appeared from the other side of the house and met their mother out front. Lynx bayed from inside the SUV.

"Who's that?" Aaron asked, nodding to a black Buick in their driveway.

Emily raised her brow. "No idea." The engine turned off and two people, a brunette young woman and an older man, got out of the car.

The woman's eyes glittered as she glanced towards the uproar coming from the SUV. The beagle scrambled to the back of the vehicle and pressed her nose against the window. At the sight of the guests, her tail went into a hesitant wag, though she kept on with her belligerent yodel.

The woman beamed at the beagle. "*Hi, Beags!*" She looked to Emily as she and the older gentleman closed in on her. "Hi, um," the woman said. "I'm sorry, we're probably intruding, but we're looking for Pete...I, uh...well, just Pete, I guess. He's...do you know...is he here?"

"Pete's here, yes," Emily said, glancing back at the house. "He's out back. Are you friends? ...Family?"

"Friends," the woman said. "Oh, um...my name is Alex."

"Albert Cole, Ma'am," the older man said, tipping his head towards her. "Pete is a dear friend of mine. As a matter of fact, the beagle singing that lovely song in your car...? Well, we know her as well."

Emily gave a distracted frown. "Ah, I see. Well, feel free to go round back, but…we're kind of on a time crunch, and come to find out, Pete is one of my best workers. …Invaluable, really. I offered to pay him, but he refused."

Albert gave a small nod and a sigh. "Yip, sounds 'bout right. That's Pete. Say, you have room for two extra workers? My granddaughter and I would be glad to pitch in."

"…Any good with a hammer?" Emily asked.

"Not a bit," Albert said.

Alex shrugged shook her head. "Sorry, no. But…I'm a fast learner!

Emily shrugged and nodded, giving a vague gesture to the house. "…The more, the merrier."

They followed Emily towards the back of the house, and were met halfway there with Pete. He blinked and shot his brow upwards as he stared at Alex. "Well you I was expecting," he said, nodding to Albert. "But you…?" he said, smiling at Alex.

Alex smirked. "Third meeting, Pete."

Pete gave a meaningful look to Albert, who nodded and gave him a half-smile. "Yeah, I told her all about our ruse to get you two kids together. You'd be surprised how understanding this gal can be."

"Apple doesn't fall far from the tree, I guess," Pete said. Alex smirked. "So," Pete continued, "did you get to meet the puppies yet?"

Alex brow shot upwards. "…*Puppies*?"

"Puppies indeed," Pete said. "Beags—uh, Lynx, that is—she's now a proud mother."

Al chuckled. "Well, bless her heart!"

Alex beamed. "...*Aw*! So *that's* why she's hanging out in a car!"

Emily nodded. "Yep. ...With a heat lamp, so the little family stays warm. We check on them often, of course. Far as we can tell, they're purebred beagles, but only time will tell." Her phone buzzed in her pocket. "Excuse me," she said, flashing a quick smile as she fished her phone out and hurried back towards the front of the house.   She paced in front of her SUV, her hand tangled up into her hair as she listened to the person on the other line. "Yes, but you don't see, I already started building. You said you could take my mother's ring as collateral. ...Yes...yes, I understand that, but...." Emily leaned against the side of her car, trying to muffle the sound of her tears as the conversation continued.

Chapter Twenty-Seven

Aaron and Lynx followed the sound of the air compressor and found Mom in the back yard. Aaron gave a weak smile, miming the act of removing her protective ear muffs. Mom powered down the air compressor, set down her drill and took off the muffs. "Yeah, Buddy? What's up?"

"I'm taking Lynx on a walk," Aaron said. "She needs a break from the pups. Did you want to come with? There's something I've been wanting to show you."

She raised her safety goggles. "Oh, uh…okay, give me just a minute…." Lynx barked an alarm to put the power tools to shame, making them both jump. They watched through the gaps in the house frame as a black Lincoln pulled into the driveway.

Mom batted some saw dust out of her hair. She avoided Aaron's gaze as she spoke to him, inciting a frown on his lips. "Um…would you mind seeing who that is, Aaron…?" she said. "If they ask for me, send them away…just, uh…tell them I'm not here."

"Uh…okay," Aaron said. "Is there something going on?"

"Nope," Mom said, a little too quickly.

Aaron stared at her for a moment, but she turned away from him and returned to her work. Aaron sighed and took Lynx to his mom's SUV. An extension cord ran from a generator to the SUV, climbed up through a window and powered the heat lamp that rested on the middle seat. Under the heat lamp was a crate, lined with one of the wool blankets, on top which the puppies wiggled and whimpered. Aaron unloaded Lynx into the crate. One of her puppies sniffed the air and yipped out a tiny bark.

Aaron smiled as Lynx circled several times and plopped down, allowing her babies to eat. "…Wish I could hang out in here with you guys," Aaron said. "You get the benefit of the generator-powered heat. I get the benefit of cold, numb fingers and an emotionally unstable mother."

"Excuse me…young man?"

Aaron shut the door and looked behind him. A plump woman with mounds of curls beamed at him. "Hello!" she said, spreading her hands outward as though she were preparing to hug Aaron. Instead she clasped her hands together and beamed at him.

Aaron gave a faint smile. "Hi….uh, something I can do for you?"

"I'm Darla Appleton," the woman said, her eyes shining with expectancy. "I'm looking for Pete…." She gave the property a sweeping view. "Is he here, dear?"

Aaron nodded to behind the woman, where Pete was approaching them.

"Oh good, you made it!" Pete said. Aaron looked on with vague interest as he leaned against the SUV.

"Peter…!" Darla said. She pulled Pete into a tight hug, jiggling her torso from side to side. "My stars!" she said, tapping her chin as she took in the sight of the house. "This place is really something! Pete tells me y'all are building this around that sweet little beagle?"

Aaron nodded. "Yup, that's right."

"Remarkable!" Darla said. "What wonderful people you must be, to go the extra mile, all for the sake of a beloved pet! Now, she is *your* dog, that's my understanding?"

"She's really more my sister's," Aaron said, "but, yeah…and she just had pu—"

"Splendid!" Darla said. "Now, uh, Pete…about the matter we discussed…?"

Pete grinned. "Glad you asked. Sit tight. I'll, uh…see to that particular matter right now."

Pete found Al and pulled him into the side yard. Voices from the back sounded, so Pete spoke in a cover tone. "Look, I want you to meet someone, Al," Pete said. "Her name is Darla Appleton. When I met you, I promised you a woman, so…*Merry Christmas*."

Al curled his lip and sighed. "Oh, Pete…kind of you, really, but I don't know about this."

Pete sighed. "Oh, come on! You can set me up, but I can't return the favor?"

Al's shoulders sank. "I…wasn't going to tell you yet, but I kind of have a thing going with a gal online."

Pete's lips twitched. "…Uh, *yeah*…that turned out to be *me*, Al, remember?"

Al frowned and gave a dismissive wave. "I know that, you stinker."

Pete chuckled. "…Just be careful. You never know about those people you meet online. Still, I'm happy for you."

"Yeah," Al said, "but the trouble is, it's on the rocks."

Pete frowned. "Oh?"

Al sighed. "Yeah. Things are iffy…we have tentative plans to meet after the new year, but…I…I just don't know….I'm just not ready to meet someone, especially not a blind date." He gave a wary glance to the back yard. "Does she know about it? I mean, does she know she's being set up?"

Pete scratched the back of his head and frowned. "Yeah, she does. Come on, Al...this will be good for you! I really think you're gonna like her. Just...give it a chance, please? I told her all about you. She is really excited to meet you...just...do this, come on, man!" He smirked and poked a finger into Al's shoulder. "Give her a shot."

"Yeah," a voice said from behind Al. His eyes widened. "Give her a shot, Al."

Al, a knot in his stomach, turned around and gaped at Darla. "*Ninja...?*"

"Hey," Darla said, putting on a mock scowl. "I'm a Flower, too, and don't you forget it!"

A slow smile spread across Al's face. He closed the gap between them, wrapped one arm around Darla's middle, cupped her cheek with his hand and pressed his lips to hers.

Darla pulled back from the kiss and tittered. She placed her palms on Al's chest and gazed up at him. "Fierce as ever, Al," she said.

Pete cleared his throat. "Um...! Well, that went...better than I expected...? I don't understand...."

Darla giggled and gave a dismissive wave. "A story for another time, Peter."

Al's bushy brow arched as he smirked at Darla. "You knew it'd be me, didn't you?"

Darla grinned and nodded. "...Guilty."

Aaron's mom approached, giving Darla a hesitant smile. "Hello...another friend of Pete's?" she said. Aaron frowned as his mom wiped her cheek with her sleeve.

"Ah, yes!" Darla said. She frowned. "Goodness, Dear, you look a mess! You're the lady of the premises, I presume? You've been working yourself to the bone!"

"All for a good cause, I assure you," Mom said, giving a shaky laugh while she wiped her eyes.

Darla shook her head and took a gentle grip on Emily's arm. "Let's just find you a nice place to sit. I'll send for coffee for your family and crew. All of you look like you need a break!"

Mom smiled. "That's, um...that's awfully nice of you."

"...Of course, dear!" Darla said. "When Mrs. Appleton sees a need, she goes the extra mile to ensure it is met!"

"Well again, thank you," Mom said. "If you'll, uh...excuse me a moment, my son wanted to show me something?" she said, looking to Aaron.

"Oh, uh, yeah," Aaron said. He nodded towards the back of the house. "Let's go."

Al and Darla shared a few more pecks, linked arms and walked towards her car. Before they went much further than the front of the house, Al turned around to see Pete giving him a quizzical smile. "Thanks, Pete," Al said, his bushy brow hanging low over his eyes. He sent a wistful smile Darla's way, then looked back to Pete. "You can't begin to understand how much I mean that."

Chapter Twenty-Eight

Mom's mouth hanged open as she gazed up at the observatory. "*Wow*, Aaron!"

Aaron cupped the back of his neck as he smiled at the ground. "Yeah, it's...nothing special. ...Not done yet, either."

Mom looked at him in her periphery and smirked. "You been sneaking out here to build this, have you?"

"Uh...*ha*, um...yes?" Aaron said, giving a sheepish grin. "And remember how we said the puppies were born just out in the middle of the forest? Yeah, that wasn't exactly the truth. They were born here."

Mom crossed her arms and arched her brow. "Well, you're just Mr. Deception lately, aren't you?"

Aaron wrinkled his brow. "Hey! It was for a good cause...a Christmas present for my little sister. ...With the money I was going to spend on my truck, thank you very much!"

"Yeah, *uh-huh*," Mom said, elbowing his ribs. She clasped her hands and sighed, looking back to the structure. "Can we check it out?"

Aaron gestured forward. "Be my guest!"

Together they climbed the steps, Mom caressing the woodwork, her eyes wide with wonder. "Beautiful craftsmanship, Aaron, really Buddy...you did a great job."

Aaron smiled. "Thank you, Mom. I had help, though."

Mom arched her brow and smiled. "...Pete?"

"Yeah," Aaron said. "He worked through the night, most of the time. Said he didn't mind doing it." They reached the top and Aaron shivered. The glow of motherly concern brewed in Mom's eyes. She took off her jacket and draped it over Aaron's shoulders.

Aaron chuckled. "…Thanks," he said, pulling her jacket closer around him.

Mom smirked and prodded his broad shoulders. "Fit you better when you were ten."

Aaron looked up at the window in the dome ceiling. "Crazy to think, isn't it? …That we're doing this, moving here, all because of a beagle."

Mom turned her attention to the wall, tracing her fingers along the wood again. "Yeah…well there's more to it than that, of course." She cleared her throat and sighed.

"You okay, Mom?" Aaron asked.

"Huh?" she said. "Oh, yeah, I just…you really did a wonderful job, Aaron. She beamed at him. "I'm proud of you. …That you would use your hard-earned money, to build this for your little sister…?"

Aaron gave a sullen shrug. "Not like I can get my license anyway."

Mom pushed out a patient sigh. "Come on, Buddy…it's not like you'll be grounded forever. And…*eventually*…you *can* get your license. But I mean, I'm just beside myself that you used your money on your sister!"

Aaron's brow furrowed with thought. "I just thought that right now, this was more important."

Mom smiled at him. "I know you don't always get along with Hannah, and I know she gets away with a lot." She sighed again and thrust her fingers through her hair.

"I'll admit that…that you were right…sort of. I go easy on her because…sometimes it's easier than to fight her on every little thing. But it's not right. It's not fair to take it out on you.

Aaron pretended to not look relieved. "It's fine, Mom."

"No, it's not," Mom said.

Aaron gave a meager shrug. We uh…we'd better get back, I guess. Not really fair to make everyone else do the work on our new house."

Mom gave a small smile. "Yeah…suppose so."

They descended the steps, Mom leading the way. Aaron heard her sigh and saw her wipe her eyes again several times.

Chapter Twenty-Nine

At the knock on her doorframe of her soon-to-be-bedroom, Hannah looked over her shoulder to her brother and returned to her hammering.

"Hey," Aaron said, strolling into the room. "Do you, uh…have any idea what's going on with Mom?"

"She's tired," Hannah said. "I'm tired, too. This is hard work, but we have to do it for Lynx."

"She was crying, I think," Aaron said, frowning as he leaned up against the wall. "It was kind of hard to tell though, because she like…never cries, but pretty sure that's what I saw."

"She probably had sawdust in her eye," Hannah said. "But if you don't think it's sawdust," she said, looking at him in her periphery, "the obvious solution is to ask *Mom* what's bothering Mom."

Aaron sighed and shook his head. "I guess that's one possible solution."

"It's the best one, too," Hannah said. Aaron rolled his eyes and returned downstairs.

After he left, a whimper and scratching noise drew Hannah to the hall, where she saw Lynx with her paws up on a baby gate Mom had dug out of their garage. "Hey, Lynx," she said, rubbing the beagle's ears. "Do you need a walk? Hold on…." She walked down the unfinished staircase and headed for the living room, where she last saw Lynx's leash draped over a saw horse by the fireplace. While she was still in the hall, Hannah saw Pete stood at the fireplace, his back to her as he polished the stones with a rag and cleaner. He glanced around him, dipped down towards the hearth below, where Hannah's mom's purse lay, and stuck his hand inside the purse's main compartment.

Hannah's stomach muscles clenched. She ducked behind a stack of several sheets of drywall and peeked over the edge of it, watching as Pete withdrew his hand from Hannah's mom's purse. He fumbled with the rag for a moment, gave the stones one last touch-up and left. Frowning, Hannah emerged from behind the drywall and looked inside her mom's purse.

Chapter Thirty

Lynx cocked her head from side to side at the chirp of a siren. Blue lights reflected against the inside paneling of the SUV. Aaron and Hannah exchanged frowns, gave the puppies they held back to Lynx, emerged from the car and ran to the driveway, where they found their mother standing in front of a squad car with her arms crossed. The officer emerged from his vehicle.

"Why is there a police officer here?" Hannah whispered to Aaron.

Aaron lifted his brow and shrugged. "*No clue!*"

"Afternoon, Ma'am," the officer said. "Been instructed to come out here and inform you and your crew that you need to vacate the premises. This is bank property."

"I *own* this property," Mom said, thrusting her finger towards the ground. "I was led to believe that this property would be *mine*."

The officer put up his hands and turned his head to the side. "Not here to argue, Ma'am. ...Just giving you a chance to move on before I'm required to use force. This is your official warning. I'll come back tomorrow. If you're not gone, I'll have to make an arrest."

Mom stood still as the officer got back into his car and left. She turned around, her face buried in her hands. Aaron sighed and nudged Hannah's arm. "Come on," he said, taking large strides towards their mother.

The crunch of his footfalls lifted her head. She hiccupped and sniffed, making haste to wipe her eyes. "Hey, Aaron," she said, plastering on a smile.

Aaron frowned. "Mom...what's going on?"

"Huh?" Mom said. "Oh, the cop...? He was just, um...heard there was some...reports of vandalism in the neighborhood...that kind of stuff, wanted to check in and see if we'd seen anything." She pushed out a heavy sigh, wiping her eyes again as she stared into the distance, away from Hannah and Aaron.

"There's no sawdust in your eyes, Mom," Hannah said.

Mom crinkled her expression. "Huh...?"

"You're *crying*, Mom," Aaron said. "What's going on?"

Mom bit her lower lip and stared at the ground, her eyes welling with fresh tears. "Oh, just..." She threw up her hands and let them drop to her sides with an air of defeat. "I...I screwed up, guys!" She shook her head and looked at Hannah. "I don't know what I was thinking. I knew how important this place was to you, Sweetheart. We didn't have quite enough to get the loan. I...gave them Grandma's ring as collateral...I thought the loan would for sure get approved." She pressed her fingertips to her temples and shook her head. "It was supposed to get us by, get us the land...for the first time in my life I didn't wait for all my ducks to be in a row, I...counted the chicks before they've hatched, and on top of it all, I just bought a painting! It was supposed to be the first decoration for the new house! I'm sorry, guys! Your mom is a screw-up!"

"So...we don't get the house?" Hannah asked.

"Oh, no, the house is ours," Mom said, smiling with spite in her eyes. "We just don't get to keep the property it's on."

"Mom," Aaron said, "I'm so sorry...."

"Oh, don't be sorry, Aaron," Mom said. "I don't deserve pity. If anything, be mad at your stupid mother who messed up your Christmas."

Aaron shook his head. "You didn't mess up Christmas, Mom. And you're not stupid." Mom gave a bitter smile.

Hannah glanced to the side and frowned. "Mom, I want gum. Can you get me a piece of gum?"

Mom narrowed her eyes, shook her head and Aaron crinkled his nose. "*What…?*" Mom said. "Hannah, I don't know if you understand…."

"Can you get me a piece of gum out of your purse?" Hannah asked. "*Please?*"

"Hannah," Mom said, her voice squeaking with hysterics, "…if you want gum, you can go find my purse and help yourself. Right now is *not the time.*"

Aaron groaned. "I'll get it."

"No!" Hannah said. "It has to be Mom! It's not…*for you.*"

Aaron stared at his sister. "*What's* not for me?"

Hannah sighed and looked up at Mom. "Just go look in your purse…*please?*"

Mom opened her mouth, closed it again and sank her shoulders. "Okay…fine…okay, I'll just go…check my purse." She shook her head in bewilderment and walked into the house.

"What's in her purse, Hannah?" Aaron asked, as they followed Mom into the living room. Hannah shrugged in response.

The clanking and whir of power tools sounded from down the hall and in the kitchen as they approached the fireplace. Emily sat down on the hearth and pulled a fat, faded white envelope out of her purse. A yellow sticky note fell from the envelope to the floor, revealing the back of the envelope, where the words GRACE FUND were written. Emily retrieved the sticky note, looked at Hannah in her periphery and pulled back the crinkled flap on the envelope. Her eyes went wide. "Oh my…!" She ran her thumb over the edges of a thick wad of bills, which were nestled inside the envelope. A swear word escaped her lips. She gasped and clapped her hand to her mouth. She looked at the note, shaking her head.

Aaron's lips parted. "Whoa...is that what I think it is?" Hannah grinned.

"There's over twelve-thousand dollars in here!" Mom said. She laughed and pressed her hand to her forehead.

"What does the note say?" Aaron asked, sitting next to his mother. "Who's it from?"

"It just, um…it just says my name," Mom said, handing the note for Aaron to see. She looked at Hannah, her eyes wet again, and furrowed her brow. "You knew about this?" Hannah nodded. Mom chirruped an emotionally-charged laugh. "Why didn't you tell me sooner? How long have you known this was in here, Hannah? Do you know where it came from?"

Hannah shrugged and forced herself to maintain eye contact as she looked at her mom. "I don't know where it came from…but I saw it yesterday when I was looking for gum," she said. "The note had your name on it, so I didn't open it, but I could see the money through the envelope. I didn't tell you because I knew it must be a Christmas surprise. You're not supposed to spoil Christmas surprises."

"Mom, you've got to go…!" Aaron said.

"…*To the bank, yes!*" Mom said, swinging her purse over her shoulder.

"I want to come with you!" Hannah said.

"Okay!" Mom said. "Let's go, let's go!"

"I'll hold down the fort," Aaron said. Lynx's bark sounded from the SUV. Aaron smirked. "…And the beagles."

Mom bit her lip and hummed. "You know…I wouldn't be surprised…heh!" She grinned and held up the cash-filled envelope. "I think I know exactly who it's from." Hannah stared up at her mother. "Mrs. Appleton!" Mom said. "It would fit…she's a wealthy lady, extremely generous." Her eyes twinkled as she tapped Hannah's forehead with the cash-stuffed envelope. "Let's keep it a secret, hmm? Can you? …It's just, usually people who do this sort of thing prefer it to remain anonymous."

Hannah nodded and gave a small smile. "…Yeah. I can keep it a secret."

Chapter Thirty-One

Aaron pulled his headphones from his ears as his mom and Hannah approached. Hannah, with Lynx on her leash, headed towards the backyard. Aaron looked to his mom. "Well...?"

Mom's face scrunched with excitement as she shrugged and grinned. "All ours!" she said. She reached into her purse and handed him the envelope. "Here!" she said.

Aaron frowned. "What's this for?" He opened the envelope and stared up at his mother. "Okay, did I miss something...?"

"That there is courtesy of your little sister," Mom said. "Oh, and of Alex—she insisted on pitching in for pizza, so I just added the ten she gave me to the rest of the cash. "You should have seen your sister at the bank, though! She talked 'em down to nine! I barely had to say a word. I'm one proud mom...that girl's got a future in business."

"That's great! But uh..." Aaron said, indicating the envelope. "Why'd you give me this...? To hold onto for you, or...?"

Mom smirked. "...For an almost sixteen-year-old's *dream*, Aaron." Aaron frowned. Mom laughed. "*It's for your truck*! To be purchased," she said, as Aaron's eyes went wide, "the day of your birthday. ...So study up, Buddy. You've got a driving test to pass next month."

Aaron gave a hesitant grin. "I...I can get my *license*?"

Mom smiled and gave a curt nod. "Yep. But you're still grounded. I'd love to let you off the hook, but what kind of parent would I be if I did that? Taking my car without my permission and driving without a license…too serious of an offense. So, get your license, get your truck, but then it's straight home after school until February the first."

Aaron rubbed the back of his neck and nodded, giving a sheepish grin. "Thanks, Mom. I mean it." He thumbed through the money and frowned. "Hey…there's something written here, inside the envelope…did you see this before?" Mom gave him a curious frown and shook her head. Aaron pushed the money aside and read, "*When empty, fill again.*"

Chapter Thirty-Two

The skill saw shrieked through the air as Pete rounded the corner. He toted a gift wrapped in metallic green paper. Tucking the gift under one arm, he waved at Alex, who released the trigger, put down the saw and pushed her safety goggles up on her head. The burly man next to her gave her a thumbs up. "Good work, Alex," he said.

"Hey!" Alex said to Pete. "Check it...turns out I'm just a *little bit* freaking *awesome* with power tools." She grinned and gestured to the pile of cut wood on the ground behind her.

"Never doubted you for a minute," Pete said. He smiled at Albert, who was perched on a cooler with his arm around Darla, the two of them engaged in conversation over coffee. He looked back to Alex. "I was wondering if you'd like to go on a walk with me...? ...Check out the observatory?"

Alex took off the goggles and set them next to the saw. "Sure! ...Sounds great!" She put on her heavy jacket and wrapped her scarf around her neck.

They strolled into the forest. Alex blew a puff of hot breath into her hands before nestling them deep into her pockets. Twigs snapped under their footfalls and a branch in her periphery nodded under the weight of a robin. "Beautiful," Alex said. She pointed to the bird and Pete smiled at the sight. "...I love how his red wings pop out from the backdrop of the withered, brown foliage," Alex said. She smirked and shrugged. "I, uh...I tend to see the world in brushstrokes."

Pete smiled. "That's really cool," he said. "...Possibly a subject for the painting you owe your grandpa?"

Alex shrugged. "Maybe. It's cool, but it doesn't really say *Albert Cole* to me, you know?"

"I get that," Pete said. They walked in silence a little longer. "So, Alex," Pete said after a while, "...you know about...my *past*. Why aren't you running?"

Alex smirked. "I wasn't fully considering dating you until Grandpa told me your story. Call me crazy, but even knowing your past, I...I couldn't possibly run. And I'm not really sure why."

Pete smiled at the ground. "Hmm. You know, I'm going to have to humbly reject your acceptance of our date, Alex."

A wave of confusion rippled Alex's face. "...*Huh*?" She smirked in spite of herself and shrugged. "I mean...you're not into me, you're not into me, that's fine, but...*wow*, I must be *really* bad at reading signals."

Pete chuckled. "You trust your grandpa," he said. "...And since he trusts me, and since he wants you to be with me, you think you're going to please the one person who understands you even a little bit by giving me a good chance. Am I right?"

Alex shook her head, but then chewed on her lip and shrugged. "I've heard crazier theories about the inner-workings of my mind." She smirked. Heat rushed to her cheeks. "But, you really should know that I *am,* um...attracted to you. ...Those gorgeous green eyes, your dimples when you smile...and your kind heart. I mean, everything you've been through and you're still this amazing person." She nodded and smiled at him. "It's really cool, Pete."

"Well...thanks," Pete said. "It means a lot to me, coming from you. But I, uh...." He scratched the back of his head and sighed. "Something's been bugging me. I'm not *that* amazing of a person. ...Because I haven't been entirely honest with Emily. Things that I *should* have been honest about. When I first met her, I let her believe I have an apartment. I suppose I was just thinking she wouldn't let me help if she thought I was homeless. And, well...it was important to me, to be able to do this for her. ...For me. But I should have given her the chance to judge that matter for herself."

"I understand," Alex said. "You needed closure, after what happened. But if I were you, I'd stop lying about who you are. You're not doing yourself any favors trying to be what other people want you to be. Fearing judgment...? It certainly won't give you that closure you're looking for."

Pete chuckled. "Yeah, well...I'll tell her *some* of who I am, but I'd prefer she doesn't know about what used to be my construction company...and about the grace fund."

Alex arched her brow. "...The envelope." She chewed her lip and smiled at him. "You gave her that money you were carrying around in the envelope."

Pete nodded. "Been planning to for quite some time now. Just needed the right moment to do it. Far as I know, she doesn't know it came from me. But her not knowing those details is part of the closure." He shrugged. "It's like—some things you just have to do...for *you*...know what I mean? It has to be done your way, because you know deep inside, it's the best choice for your life." Alex gave a small smile and nodded. "Which brings me back around to why I rejected your acceptance of our date," Pete said. "I mean…Alex…do you even want to date anyone at *all* right now?"

Alex shrugged. "I don't know. I mean…of course I do. Yeah, I do. …I think."

Pete's gaze met hers with a gentle force. "Here's my theory. You may or may not want romance, but what you *do* want is companionship. Someone to…fully understand you, to fully see you for who you are. To not cast you in some role, to not push you into a mold for which you're not fitted."

Alex stared at him and laughed. "Okay, what, were you a shrink in your past life?"

Pete gave a wry grin. "I've…had a lot of experience with, uh, how do I put this…*reading people*….?" He gave a sheepish shrug. "…If you know what I mean."

Alex gave a slow nod and smiled. "Ah, yes, that's right…I see." She drew in a deep breath and held it, looking upwards at Pete. Her shoulders sank as she exhaled. "Can I tell you something?" Pete nodded. "I…do want to meet someone," Alex said. "I mean, I want to fall in love, get married. I want babies, I want companionship, just like you said. And here's what really scares me…I don't know if I'll ever find that." She shrugged and stared off into the woods, her eyes shining with tears. "I don't know if I'm just…meant to be alone, for the rest of my life. My family wants me to get married, and because I'm not, they think there's something wrong with me…you know, Alex, the *zany artist,* doomed to be a waitress *for the rest of her life*…and what scares me the most…?" she said, tears trickling down her cheeks. "I'm starting to think they're right."

Pete sighed. His face wrinkled into a sympathetic remorse as he wrapped his arms around Alex in a hug. Alex returned the hug, welcoming that of Pete's and the warmth it offered in the chilled air. She didn't want it to end, but after a moment, Pete stepped back and clutched her shoulder as he looked at her. "You know, your grandfather is a very generous man, but, I don't have to tell you that. I mean, for heaven's sake, I tried to steal from him and he gives me money and ends up trying to set me up with his granddaughter!" Alex gave a teary laugh, dousing the air in front of her with a burst of white breath.

"...But anyway," Pete continued, "my point is, your grandpa is good at meeting people where they are, without question. But *you're* forgetting to meet someone where they are. You're forgetting *yourself*, Alex." Alex rubbed her nose and frowned. "You're forgetting to meet yourself, where you are," Pete continued, "and by that I mean you're forgetting to be *patient* with yourself. Your family, they've taught you to be anything but patient, because in a sense, they've lost patience with you." He shrugged. "You haven't done what everyone's expected you to do. Trust me, I know a thing or two about that." His eyes glazed over with a sad light. "People aren't kind to you when you don't follow their notions of what the rules of life ought to be. Just, uh...just don't let your grace fund supply run low...with them, or with yourself."

Alex wiped away the tears from her cheeks. "You're uh...you're good guy, Pete," she said, giving an exuberant nod.

Pete smiled at the ground and nodded. "Whoever you end up with, if that's what you even want, well, he's lucky to have you, whoever he is. Promise me you'll be picky. A girl like you...you can afford to be picky. Make it on your own terms. Make it your move, not someone else's. Don't settle."

Alex swallowed hard and smiled through her tears. "Thanks, Pete. But just so you know, if it ends up being you…it's anything but settling."

Pete smiled and offered her his hand. "Friends…?"

Alex pulled her lips inward and shook his hand. "…Friends." Her eyes twinkled. "…For now."

Pete chuckled. "…Alright, fair enough."

Alex thrust her hands in her pockets forward, making the bottom of her jacket lift. "So," she said, grinning like a little girl as she plopped her hands back to her sides. "…Who's the gift for?"

"Ah, yes," Pete said, smiling at the gift in his hands. "This…." Mischief twinkled in his eyes. "I was hoping you could give the Davenports a Christmas present." Alex frowned as he handed her the gift. "Open it," Pete said.

Alex cocked her head and frowned, pointing at the present. "You want me to give the *Davenports* a present, and then you hand *me* a present? I…"

Pete chuckled. "Just open it."

Alex gave a hesitant smirk. "Okay…" With a nervous chuckle, she tore into the paper. She took in a wavering breath, blinked, and exhaled with a smile as a familiar banana painting stared back at her.

"Don't get too excited," Pete said. "It belongs to the Davenports. Or, it will, when you sell it to them."

Alex gave him a watery-eyed look. "…Okay, now I'm *really* confused."

Pete rubbed the back of his neck and smiled at her. "Let's see if I can catch you up to speed." His eyes swiveled upwards in thought. "Well, let's see, the painting *was* yours, when you painted it. Then you gave it to your sister-in-law. Then she pawned it. Then your grandpa told me about it. Then I bought it, and gave it to you, but you decided to not keep it, of course...." He caught her gaze and grinned. "You decided to sell it to the Davenports." Alex smirked. Pete fished in his pocket, pulled out and pressed an envelope into her palm. "...Cash from the Davenports, plus you'll find a business card in there. ...Owner of the pawn shop. Told him I knew the artist. He's a collector, pays top dollar, and he's very interested in your work."

Alex shook her head as more tears slipped from her eyes. "I don't know how to repay you...!"

Pete smiled. "So don't."

A twig snapped from behind them. Pete turned to see Aaron. "Hey," Aaron said. He grinned and gestured for them to follow him. "We have a surprise for everyone."

Chapter Thirty-Three

The smell of oregano, pepperoni and mulled cider spiced the frigid air as the Davenports and their guests gathered under the eaves in the backyard. Anticipation gripped the air. A half empty cardboard box of ornaments Al had brought sat on the frozen ground, next to a young noble fir. An unplugged extension cord ran from the foot of the tree to an outlet located near the corner of the house. Hannah and Darla extracted bulbs from the box and conferred with each other the perfect placement of each one.

Al scratched his head and frowned at Emily. "Back in my day," he said, "we took Christmas trees indoors before decorating 'em."

Emily shrugged and smiled. "This one's meant to be right where it is."

After some time, Darla looked towards Alex, who stood near the outlet. She cupped her hands around her mouth. "All set, dear!"

Alex plugged in the cord. A soft glow engulfed the tree and illuminated the ground around it. Amidst a chorus of *oohs* and *ahhs*, every face there turned to admire the sight. Al gave a low whistle, looked at Emily and nodded. "I see what you mean."

Hannah, her arms crossed as she shivered, stepped back and surveyed the tree. Aaron, with Lynx on her leash, stepped up beside her. "Not bad, little sister. I don't think we should put any presents under it, but, still…it looks good."

Hannah looked at him. "It's about to get even better." Aaron gave her questioning frown, but their mother's spirited call for them to head inside to eat diverted his attention.

Alex and Al broke out into an off-key rendition of *Deck the Halls*, making the others either cringe or laugh. The song tapered off as everyone was seated on the saw-dust ridden floor, and was replaced by the sound of puppy whimpers as the babies ate and explored their crate.

"Sorry," Emily said, glancing at Darla in her periphery as she indicated the pizza boxes and paper plates. "I know this isn't very fancy, especially after all the help and support all of you have been."

"...*Nonsense!*" Darla said. "This is a *feast,* fit for a *Queen*! Though I don't suppose you have any ketchup...?" Emily wrinkled her brow and frowned.

"Gotcha covered," Pete said. He reached into his jacket, retrieved a bottle of ketchup, and tossed it to Darla. He grinned. "I figured you'd be asking for some at some point." Alex laughed.

"Oh, splendid!" Darla said, opening the bottle.

"Ketchup on your *pizza*...?" Hannah said, making a face. "That's incredibly *bizarre!*"

"Oh, Sweetheart," Darla said, dismissively tossing her hand to the air. "...Dare to be *different!*"

Al grinned and patted Darla's knee. "...Wouldn't have her any other way."

"This is perfect, Emily, thank you," Alex said through the cider steam, as it warmed the tip of her chilled nose.

Emily smiled. "You're quite welcome."

Aaron plopped two pieces of pizza onto a plate. "Pete," he said, handing him the plate.

Pete smiled. "Thank you, Aaron."

Lynx licked her chops and sniffed the air through the crate. Hannah smiled at Aaron as he fed the beagle a piece of pepperoni.

Alex peered outside the window at the radiant tree. "It really does look great out there," she said. "...A beacon of warmth and hope, amongst the dreary winter." A crease of wonder met her brow as a fleck of white floating downwards near the tree caught her eye. She pointed. "Oh, Gosh! *It's starting to snow!*"

Emily craned her neck and scrutinized the backyard, and the others gathered and looked out the windows and backdoor. "Wow! Oh, how *perfect!*" Emily said. Aaron glanced at his sister, who gave a thin knowing smile. They watched with awe as a dusting of white kissed the branches, lights and ornaments on the tree.

"How *gorgeous!*" Alex said.

Pete stuck his hands into his pockets and poked his head out the backdoor. He blinked as whirling snowflakes brushed against his eyelids and caressed his cheeks with pinpricks of cold. "Really coming down quickly!"

Aaron smirked. "Nature wanted to decorate too, I guess."

"Oh, it's *wonderful,*" Emily said. She crossed her arms and gave a wistful sigh. "I've always loved snow. Everything is subject to it. ...The mucky dirt, the plants, the cars...when it snows, everything is made equal, and is made equally *beautiful.*"

They all murmured their agreements then watched in silence as the backyard transformed into a winter wonderland. The snow distorted the white twinkle of each light on the tree, spreading the glow throughout the dollops of white like paint on a canvas. After a while, a branch bobbed under the snow's weight and an ornament fell. Aaron grabbed Hannah's arm, stopping her from going out to fix it.

"Let it be," he whispered. "Just for a moment." Hannah frowned but relented, and watched with uneasy eyes as snow gathered on the ornament's top.

Alex leaned down to Hannah's ear and smiled. "It looks at home, there, doesn't it? The ornament, I mean."

Hannah put a step's distance between her and Alex and furrowed her brow. "It should be on the tree. That's where I put it."

"But maybe it prefers to be on the ground," Alex said. "...Are you really going to force it to be somewhere else?"

Hannah frowned. "That's ridiculous. Ornaments can't want things. They don't have *brains*."

"Then, by all means," Alex said, a gentle tease to her tone as she gestured to the backyard. "Go out there and put it back, right where it should be. But if you walk out there, you'll leave a trail of footprints in that perfect, unblemished white blanket. And, I mean, who knows if the falling snow will cover your tracks? It could slow down or stop *any minute*." Hannah glanced to one side.

"Ah yes, and consider this, young lady," Al said. "Kinetic energy, gravity...*science* did this. It would be irresponsible of you to intervene. Don't you think?" Aaron smirked as he glanced at Hannah in his periphery.

Hannah's gaze shifted to the ground, then she sighed and stared at the snow-covered ornament. She could just see a swirly segment of a glitter line on the ornament's side as it glistened under the span of the tree's lights. Soon, the snow covered the ornament in its entirety, conquering the manmade object and rendering it a white blob, like everything else the snow touched. "I'll put it back," she said. "...After the snow melts." Aaron exchanged covert grins with Alex and her grandfather.

Pete placed his hand on Alex's shoulder. Alex smiled. His touch sent a jolt through her skin and sent her stomach into a fluttering frenzy. Pete gestured towards the snowy scene. "How about *this* for your painting, huh?"

Alex narrowed her eyes in thought and shook her head. "Nah. It's close, though...but not quite."

After a while, they all broke away from the windows and door and returned to their meal.

"Oh!" Emily said, between bites of pizza. "...Before I forget, you're all invited to come to our apartment in the city tomorrow night, for Christmas Eve dinner."

"Oh, thank you!" Alex said. "...But we uh, we have our family dinner." She smiled at her grandpa.

"I have a prior engagement as well," Darla said, squirting a healthy dose of ketchup on her pizza. "But I thank you kindly for the invitation."

"Pete will stay," Aaron said, giving a jovial grin to the man. "...Won't you?"

"I'd love to," Pete said. "But I've already been invited to the Rothman residence, to join Alex, Al and their family for dinner."

"Oh...?" Emily said. "Well, that sounds nice."

"Um, Mom...?" Aaron said. "The *surprise*...?"

Emily, her eyes lighting up with acknowledgment, rushed to swallow the bite in her mouth. "Yes!" she said. She nodded to the puppy crate and smiled. "I've discussed it at large with both Aaron and Hannah, and we all agreed.

When they're ready to leave Lynx, we want each of you to take home a beagle puppy…our gift to each of you."

Alex's eyes twinkled as she cast a love-struck look to the box. "Oh…! How *wonderful!*"

"Well!" Darla said, pressing a hand to her chest. "…Mighty generous of you! I couldn't be more pleased! Thank you, thank you indeed!"

Al wheezed a chuckle. "I was just a boy the last time someone gave me a puppy for Christmas! All it needs is a big red bow round its neck!"

Pete gave a curt nod and smile. "…Best Christmas present I've received in a good long while. Thank you, Emily. This, ah…changes my plans for my living situation, of course, but…change can be a good thing." He smiled at Alex, who beamed in return.

Emily beamed. "It's the least we could do."

"This calls for a toast," Al said, lifting his cider cup to the air." The others did the same. "To the furry vagabond," he said, "who has, in a way, brought us all together, and who is at last home, just in time for Christmas… To…ah, uh…" He trailed off and looked at a loss at what to say next.

Aaron lifted his cup higher. "To *The Christmas Beagle!*"

Al chuckled and nodded. "Yes! To The Christmas Beagle!"

They each touched their cups with their neighbors. "To The Christmas Beagle!" each said.

"…And to her pups!" Al added. They all sipped from their cider cups and continued eating.

"Excuse me, please," Emily said, "...I'll just take out these pizza boxes to the dumpster."

Aaron got to his feet. "I'll help you, Mom."

Alex, Al and Darla played with the puppies while Hannah hopped up from the ground, retrieved a puzzle box from her back pack and sat down next to a propane heater in the corner. Pete brushed off some sawdust from his boot and strolled over to where Hannah was sitting.

Hannah gave him a sidelong glance. "My mom was mean to you," she said. "You're the window-washer."

Pete gave a small smile. "Yeah...you remember me, huh?" Hannah nodded. Pete furrowed his brow. "...Think your mom does?"

Hannah shook her head. "No. She doesn't remember things like I do. She's too busy being a mom."

"Ah...yeah," Pete said. He heaved a sigh and stared at his palms.

Hannah put another piece into place. "I won't tell her who you are," she said. "Because if I did, it would make you feel awkward. Awkward isn't a fun feeling. When people stare at me, I feel awkward." Her eyes swiveled upwards as she sent a sharp glare to Pete.

"Ah...yes," he said, taking a step back from her. "Sorry."

"It's okay," Hannah said. "You don't make me feel *too* awkward." She squished her lips to one side. "I remember Alex, too, from before. I saw her in the bathroom at the mall. She's smart. She talks to herself. And she's good at painting. I like her."

Pete smirked. "Me, too." He looked over his shoulder at Alex, who sipped cider while she chatted with her grandfather about the banana painting. Their eyes met for a moment, and they both smiled. Alex broke her gaze as her grandfather spoke again. Pete smiled towards the ground in thought then looked back at Hannah. "…Whatcha working on?"

Hannah kept her eyes glued to her work. "…Puzzle." She sighed and stared with regret at the hole the missing piece, if she had it, would fill. Wistfulness filled her heart as she envisioned the piece appearing out of thin air.

Pete nodded to it. "Ah…you're missing a piece."

Hannah looked up at Pete. "I know. And I know staring at it won't make the piece appear. I was doing wishful thinking. I was stupid to think it might work. It's not logical at all."

Pete rummaged in his pocket, smiled, and produced a faded puzzle piece. Part of the image had peeled up from the cardboard backing. Hannah frowned as he pressed the puzzle piece into her hand. She gave him a hesitant glance, and at his smile, she pushed the piece into the open space. Despite its disrepair, it was a perfect fit. A slow smile spread across Hannah's face as she looked to Pete. "…Nothing wrong with wishful thinking, Hannah. Sometimes logic fails. That's where miracles come into play."

Hannah's smile faltered. "You've been around my family before. It makes sense that there'd be a chance that you'd end up with the puzzle piece, and it makes sense that there'd be a chance that you'd give it back to us, too." She pushed her lips to one side and narrowed her eyes in thought as she looked to Pete and shrugged. "I guess we could call it…a *miraculous* probability." Pete nodded and chuckled. Hannah got up from the chair and walked over to Lynx, let her out of the crate, and sat down on the hearth.

Lynx sat at her feet and stared up at her with pleading eyes as she ate another slice of pizza.

Al stuck his hands into his pockets, gave Pete a meaningful glance, and shuffled away from his granddaughter. Pete swallowed hard and approached Alex. She beamed at him. "Hey," she said. "Having fun?"

Pete swallowed hard and enclosed her chilled hands with his own. A rush of excitement prickled within each of them. Confusion, then warmth met her face as Alex looked up at Pete. His dimples greeted her. "We never did finish our walk," he said.

Alex nodded. "Yeah...okay." Her stomach flipped. They laced their fingers together and walked out to the backyard. The mind fog reduced Alex's stomach and limbs to gelatin.

As they neared the decorated, snow-covered tree, Pete spun Alex towards him. She shrieked a laugh, but grew solemn as he nestled his palm to the small of her back. His eyes glittered as he tilted her chin upwards. Alex closed her eyes and awaited his lips. But they didn't come. "Okay," Pete said. Alex opened her eyes. "Your move," Pete said. "...Your life, your move. You need to decide if—" Alex smirked, rolled her eyes and kissed him. He kissed her back and cradled her head as the snow peppered their hair and shoulders.

Lynx's bark broke their embrace. They looked behind them, where Hannah stood near the eaves of the house while Lynx turned a patch of snow yellow. Hannah looked determinedly at the ground. Alex and Pete exchanged wry grins, and returned to the house hand-in-hand. Hannah followed after them before too long.

Emily returned, shaking the cold from her shoulders as she warmed her hands by the propane heater. She frowned at Pete. "This has been bugging me since we first met, but do I…*know* you from somewhere?"

Pete hid a smile and shrugged. "Oh, could be—my guess is from the mall. I work there."

Emily narrowed her eyes and frowned. "Ah…yeah, heh…that's probably it. Thank you again…for all you've done. It's been a huge blessing, truly."

"My pleasure," Pete said. An ear-splitting woof made them jump, and Pete laughed as he looked to see Lynx's paws up on the hearth as she asked Hannah for more pepperoni.

One of the puppies, like a worm with a wagging tail, inched along over the bar on the bottom of the crate's opening and squeaked as he sniffed the air. Al wheezed a laugh at the sight. "Alright, I have dibs on *that* ambitious little monkey!"

Emily smiled and looked at Pete. "Well, I think I'm going to start rounding up my kids and head back to the apartment for the night. Thank you again for all your help! If I don't see you before…Merry Christmas, Pete."

Pete inclined his head towards her. "…Merry Christmas, Ma'am."

"Mom?" Aaron said. Emily turned to see her son, his arms full of firewood, kindling and newspapers. He smiled. "How 'bout we stay a little longer and try out that fireplace?"

Emily gave a hesitant smile, but Hannah popped up from the hearth. "I'll help!" Hannah said.

Emily shrugged and nodded. "Okay…a fire it is."

Lynx's head rotated from side to side, a curious glint in her eyes as she watched Aaron and Hannah arrange the wood. Pete assisted with the newspaper, twisting the torn shreds into tight bunches before nestling them in with the wood and kindling.

"Be careful, now," Al said. "Don't ever leave a fire unattended, kids." He concealed his mouth behind his hand and leaned into Emily. "I'd hate to see history repeat itself, that's all."

Darla gasped. "Oh, Al! What a dreadful thing to say!"

Al shrugged. "I just don't want to see all this hard work put to waste! You never know…tempting fate, and all that! And anyway, I'm not saying anything that any of us hasn't been thinking all along. It had to be said. That's all." Darla scoffed and rolled her eyes.

Emily's brow shot upwards but she gazed at her children, she beamed and gave a dismissive wave. "Nah…I wouldn't worry. This time around, things will be different."

Al put up his hands and offered an apologetic frown. "Honestly, Emily, I didn't mean to ruffle any feathers."

"No, it's okay," Emily said. "No harm done."

"Alright," Pete said to Aaron. He gestured to the wood stacked in the fireplace. "…Perfect teepee style. Now you're ready to light it."

Aaron's face flushed and he clutched the back of his neck. "Right. I, uh, kind of forgot that part. I don't have anything to light it."

Pete frowned, checked his pockets and produced a small blue lighter with a chip towards its top. Hannah wrinkled her nose. "Does that even *work*?"

Pete thrust his thumb down the flint and a lick of flame appeared. Aaron saw the mirth in his face he eyed Hannah in his periphery and lit one of the balls of newspaper near the bottom of the alcove. Hannah pulled her lips to one side and watched as the flames climbed up the pieces of kindling. "Yes," Pete said. He chuckled. "I'd say it works just fine." Aaron smirked.

At the flames' first crackle, Hannah sucked in a sharp breath through her nose and scooted further down the hearth, away from the flames. Meanwhile, the tantalizing smell of smoke and cedar beckoned everyone else closer to the fire's side. Al wheezed a small, delighted chuckle at the sight of Alex and Pete's adjoined hands.

Lynx sniffed the air. Though a chill crept up Hannah's arms and legs, she kept her distance from the flames. She looked at Lynx as the beagle hopped up next to her. She draped her arm over the beagle's body, but as Lynx shivered, Hannah stared at her, her face twisted in concern. She wrapped the beagle in a hug and moved closer to the fire. Lynx squeaked out a yawn and curled up into a ball on Hannah's lap. Warmth enveloped both of them.

Alex beamed at Hannah and Lynx, huddled together by the fireplace, each offering the other what they longed for the most. She looked over her shoulder and exchanged glances with her grandpa. He acknowledged her with a meaningful smile. They had found the subject of his promised painting.

Outside, the snow continued to fall in silent wonder. Inside, the fire popped, but Hannah put her fingers to work, drawing circles onto the velvet surface of Lynx's ears. Lynx trained her soulful eyes up at Hannah, stood and nuzzled her arm. Bliss bubbled over on Hannah's face as she pulled Lynx up into her arms and buried her face into her furry neck. "Merry Christmas, Lynx," she whispered. "And welcome home."

About the Author

S.E. Eaton graduated from Trinity Lutheran College in 2007 with a BA in Biblical Studies. She is the author of "The Voiceless", "Compulse" and is working on a middle-grade fantasy series and a stand-alone romance novel. She lives in Washington State with her husband Steven and their beagle Emmie Lou. In her spare time she enjoys traveling, playing trivia board games and consuming copious amounts of coffee.

Contact S.E. Eaton:

authorseeaton@gmail.com

https://seeatonblog.wordpress.com

Made in the USA
Lexington, KY
30 November 2016